MURDER ON THE TRINITY

BOOK THREE: SCHOOL'S OUT

www.CreativeTexts.com

Creative Texts Publishers products are available at special discounts for bulk purchase for sale promotions, premiums, fund-raising, and educational needs. For details, write Creative Texts Publishers, PO Box 50, Barto, PA 19504, or visit www.creativetexts.com

Murder on the Trinity: Book Three: School's Out
by Sue Land

A COLD WEST BOOK

Published by Creative Texts Publishers
PO Box 50
Barto, PA 19504
www.creativetexts.com

Copyright 2020 by Sue Land
All rights reserved
Cover photo modified and used by license.
Cover Copyright 2020 by Creative Texts Publishers, LLC

This book or parts thereof may not be reproduced in any form, stored in a retrieval system, or transmitted in any form by any means—electronic, mechanical, photocopy, recording, or otherwise—without prior written permission of the publisher, except as provided by United States of America copyright law.

The following is a work of fiction. Any resemblance to actual names, persons, businesses, and incidents is strictly coincidental. Locations are used only in the general sense and do not represent the real place in actuality.

ISBN: 978-1-64738-013-7

# MURDER ON THE TRINITY
# BOOK THREE: SCHOOL'S OUT

CREATIVE TEXTS PUBLISHERS

Barto, PA

## **TABLE OF CONTENTS**

```
CHAPTER 1  ..........................   1
CHAPTER 2  ..........................  22
CHAPTER 3  ..........................  41
CHAPTER 4  ..........................  50
CHAPTER 5  ..........................  55
CHAPTER 6  ..........................  69
CHAPTER 7  ..........................  80
CHAPTER 8  ..........................  94
CHAPTER 9  .......................... 104
CHAPTER 10 .......................... 121
CHAPTER 11 .......................... 132
CHAPTER 12 .......................... 138
CHAPTER 13 .......................... 146
CHAPTER 14 .......................... 152
CHAPTER 15 .......................... 161
CHAPTER 16 .......................... 172
CHAPTER 17 .......................... 180
```

## **CHAPTER 1**

Walking down the steps of the Liberty Texas Courthouse, Sheriff Jonathan Lawrence wasn't sure he was anywhere near ready to face the day ahead. His day had started like any other day, with a phone call, only this time it was from the Governor of Texas. The call came as somewhat of a surprise but the fact that the Governor had called to request his help came as an even bigger surprise. He wasn't thrilled about the request but he knew that his delaying getting started wouldn't make it any easier. As his mother often told him when he was a boy, "All you need to do is to hitch up your pants like a big boy and get'er done."

Two hours later, Jonathan was finally able to relax. He had successfully granted the Governor's request to give a commencement speech and it had not been as tough as he had thought it would be. Just the idea of standing in front of one hundred and twelve graduating high school students would put knots in most people's craw. Today's subject, the Trinity River, made it even harder. All these teenagers had grown up around the river. They knew the river.

The Governor had been scheduled to give the speech but urgent government business had required a last-minute change in his schedule. With no one else to turn to, Governor Browning had called the Sheriff, his one and only friend in this area. Of course, the Governor was well-accustomed to giving speeches but still yet, Jonathan could not help but wonder if there really had been some urgent business or if for some reason, he just didn't want to give this one.

Following his speech, Jonathan took the time to meet with members of the high school's teaching staff when suddenly a shrill scream interrupted the conversations. Everyone but the Sheriff turned and ran toward the opposite side of the schoolhouse away from where the scream originated.

Rounding the corner of the high school building, the Sheriff discovered the cause of the screaming. A man's body lay on the ground, next to a rock birdbath, in a puddle of blood that surrounded the man's head. Jonathan's first impression was the man had fallen from the top of the building, hitting his head on the birdbath.

Looking up at the roof of the three-story building Jonathan's eyes followed an imaginary line leading down to the body. There wasn't any doubt that the man had taken a dive off the roof but the question was whether it was a suicide, an accident, or whether or not perhaps he was pushed? Those were the sixty-four thousand-dollar questions that the CSI guys would have to answer.

Dr. Robert Dean had been in the coroner's lab when the body in question was delivered. Dean was around six feet tall with a muscular build, snow-white hair with streak of black running through it. Hazel eyes that had seen too many harsh realities in his sixty years on earth. Dean was successful enough not to put on airs and had little patience for others who did. When Jonathan walked in, Dean was clearly irritated by the sheriff's presence.

"Sheriff Lawrence, you need to give this lab enough time to perform a proper autopsy." He snapped.

"Sorry Doc," Jonathan responded. "But, my Chief Deputy Skywolf and my assistant Lillian are still on their honeymoon. That leaves me to do follow up."

Dean tried not to smile as he gave the Sheriff one last dig. "That means they aren't around for you to harass, so you're stuck with me."

"That's just about it." Jonathan agreed and then asked, "Got anything besides the fact the poor guy bashed his skull in when he fell?"

Shaking his head Dean said, "There is one thing more."

Wanting Dean to hurry things along, Jonathan urged, "And?"

"The preliminary exam isn't complete, but I can tell you that the blow to his skull did not kill him." He held a plastic bag out to Jonathan and continued, "If not, what did you might ask?"

Jonathan took the bag, studying its contents as Dean continued.

"This six-inch serrated knife inserted beneath his heart is what killed him. The knife was lodged in your dead guy's ribcage, piercing his heart. Haven't tested the blood on it yet but, I'd say with a ninety-nine per cent accuracy, the knife is what killed the guy."

Moving over to stand next to his John Doe's body, Dean continued, "There's nothing outstanding about the man's looks, white Caucasian with brown hair, blue eyes, weighing about one hundred seventy to one hundred eighty pounds. There were no wounds on his body to indicate any previous altercations. And, to complicate things, John Doe didn't have one single piece of paper on his person giving any clues to his identity."

Jonathan didn't like the way things were shaping up but before he could make any kind of reply Dean added, "At first look, you see a head bashed in by something blunt and hard. Considering the blood at the drinking fountain, you'd think that's what killed him when he took his swan dive off the roof. However, when you roll him over, you see the knife. My question is why would anyone throw the guy off the roof after knifing him? It's beyond me. That's your bandwagon."

"Yea." Was Jonathans' only reply before he asked, "No hit on John Doe's fingerprints, I assume?"

Shaking his head, Dean reminded Jonathan, "I know the drill, Sheriff. As soon as I know, you'll know."

Jonathan removed his phone from his belt and pushed his office number. When a young unfamiliar voice answered, it took a moment for him to remember the change. Janie Stewart was the temporary replacement until Lillian came back from her honeymoon.

Not returning her happy greeting, he barked "Janie, get a hold of Chester Woods and tell him to come to the office ASAP. Get CSI back out to the high school. I want the school's roof and the area right above the water fountain, swept. They are to bring in anything they find: gum wrappers, toothpicks, whatever. I don't care what it is. I want it in the lab and gone over with a fine-tooth comb. And, get me some photos of the damn crime scene." With those final words, he disconnected and with long strides and not so much as a "by your leave", he walked out of the coroner's lab. Jonathan knew he needed coffee. It couldn't make the shitty day any better, but it could give his brain a needed boost.

A short drive and fifteen minutes later, he entered the Travis Street Café, the owner Mary Wilson gave Jonathan her standard warm greeting. It didn't matter how bad Mary's day was going, she always had a smile and a cheery greeting for her customers.

Jonathan returned her greeting with a forced but equally cheery, "Morning Mary." Sitting down at the counter he said, "I'll have my usual coffee and one of your homemade fried pies to go, please."

Shaking her head, Mary scolded, "Sheriff, you keep eating my pies and you're going to be sporting a pot belly just like Pete Stringer's." Placing a steaming cup of black coffee in front of him, Mary's smile evaporated into a frown as she asked, "Would you happen to have a few minutes that you could spare me today?"

Jonathan wanted to say no but couldn't. Mary had more than her share of heartbreaks. One of them was Eric, her sixteen-year-old son, who was currently serving fifteen years for abduction and assault.

"Always for you Mary." He told her, adding, "'Come by and see me at the office when you can get away from here."

The smile was back on Mary's face again as she said, "I can take a break in a couple of hours. Thank you, Sheriff."

Picking up his coffee and pie, Jonathan reminded her, "Mary, I've known you for a few years now. I've told you to call me Jonathan. We're friends. Remember?"

Mary's smile widened "I'll remember. Thank you, Jonathan."

Ten minutes later, walking into the Sheriff's office in the Liberty County courthouse Jonathan was startled by Janie Stewart, a beautiful, young brunette in her early twenties hurrying toward him. The girl had more energy and bounce than anyone and constantly oozed it. Smiling at her, Jonathan kept on walking as Janie followed him into his office. Sitting down behind his desk he said, "You are on fire about something, so let me have it."

Handing a small white slip of paper to him, Janie told him, "An FBI guy named Sheridan has called for you twice. Says you are to call ASAP." Having delivered the message Janie hurried back out to her reception desk.

Looking at the time of the calls, the first at seven a.m., the second thirty minutes ago, Jonathan's brow deepened into a frown as he dialed Phil Sheridan's number, his age-old warning itch began to nibble on his spine. When Sheridan answered, he greeted him with, "If it was so damned important why didn't you call my cell?"

"Well, morning to you too, Sheriff Lawrence." Before Jonathan could reply Sheridan asked, "How's my Sammy? And why aren't you still on your honeymoon?"

Janie chose then to stick her head around the door to inform him, "Chester's here Sheriff."

Nodding, Jonathan held his right index finger up, indicating he wanted her to have Chester wait while he finished his call.

"Sam is doing great and the honeymoon was cut short when she accepted an assignment. What has you in a tailspin to talk to me?"

"Your John Doe inquiry set off bells and sirens. I'm in Austin, should be there in your quaint little town in a few hours."

"When did you get approved for active duty? Last I heard you were still playing the wounded hero bit?"

"I still am but, this is special circumstance." Sheridan replied.

"What kind of special circumstance?" Jonathan questioned, the itch growing.

"Your John Doe is Henri Gustaf, a retired KGB operative." Sheridan told him and paused for Jonathan's reaction; he wasn't disappointed.

"What the hell is a retired KGB operative doing on the slab in my morgue?"

"Well, I'd say right about now… being cut open by your favorite lab doc, Dean." Sheridan managed to say without choking on laughter at his own joke.

"Ha, ha, very funny Sheridan." Came Jonathan's humorless reply.

"Couldn't resist, ol' boy. Gustaf was brought out of retirement six months ago by the Russian Secret Service. They had a special op for him"

"What kind of special op?" Jonathan interjected, his irritation growing at the slow speed of Sheridan's unraveling tale.

"A few decades ago, Russia implanted some sleepers in the U.S. It seems Gustaf was the head of that little operation. He was activated to find these sleepers, deactivate them and send them back to Russia."

"So how did he end up here in my town? Dead?" was Jonathan's only question that seems Sheridan was fully prepared to answer. He was also prepared for the fact that Jonathan was not going to like that answer.

"Gustaf's orders were also to eliminate anyone that did not want to return to Russia after all these years. So far, there have been two killed with a trail leading back to Gustaf. It seems wherever Mr. Gustaf goes death follows. First time it's been his."

"That still does not tell me why my town?"

"Oh hell, Jonathan, you know the answer to that question as well as me." Sheridan answered with a sigh of impatience.

"Yeah," Jonathan replied, adding, "We've got a sleeper."

"So, I need to make a positive eye identification. Like I said, I'll be there in a couple of hours and I expect you to buy me dinner."

"Sure, got some of the best barbeque you ever tasted."

"Sounds great, mouth's watering now." Sheridan answered.

Hanging up, Jonathan buzzed Janie on his intercom, "Janie, tell Chester to come in."

A few seconds later, Deputy Chester Woods walked through the door with a cheery greeting, "Morning Sheriff."

Motioning for Chester to have a seat, Jonathan returned his greeting, "Morning Chester, how's your wife, Vickie, feeling today?"

"Oh, she is feeling much better Sheriff. The doctor tells us that the morning sickness should subside in another week or so. That made her feel somewhat better."

"Glad to hear that, you give her my regards." He told Chester before bringing him up on the current morning's events, it only took a few minutes. Chester sat quietly, absorbing what Jonathan said to him and by the time Jonathan finished, he knew his deputy was totally confused. It was evident when Chester asked, "I don't understand, why would some KGB operative settle here? What do we have that they would want?"

"That's a good question, Chester. Maybe the FBI will be able to shed some light on that." Jonathan knew he was not doing much to ease Chester's confusion and, if truth were told, it didn't do much for him either.

"Why off the high school roof?" Chester struggled to suppress a small twisted smile at the silliness of his question.

"Seems feasible that," Jonathan could almost bet money on what Chester was thinking, "he was meeting someone that worked there and what better place to talk privately?"

"And that someone pushes our guy off the roof after sticking a six-inch blade in him?" Chester asked, trying to absorb what he considered the stupidity of it all.

"Yeah, which means we have a teacher, a staff member, or a student that is a killer." was Jonathan's reply. Pushing the intercom button for Janie again, Jonathan told her, "Janie, get a hold of Judge Robinson's clerk and get me a search warrant for the high school's personal records."

Janie's quick reply of "Yes Sir," was followed by, "Sheriff there is a Lucas Wilson waiting to see you."

Standing, Jonathan said, "Send him in." Walking over to his office door, he opened it, greeting Lucas with, "This is a welcome surprise."

Lucas stood about five-feet-eleven-inches tall, weighing about one hundred and sixty-five pounds, with reddish-brown hair that reached just past his collar curling at the ends. He had blue eyes and a small, reddish-brown mustache. The whole picture was that of a Cowboy, from his cowboy boots to his tight-fitting blue jeans and Stetson hat.

Gripping Jonathan's outstretched hand, Lucas returned the greeting. "Thought I'd stop in and see if married life has changed you any."

"Not yet but, give it time." Jonathan said as he turned to Chester, "you remember my deputy, Chester."

Nodding Lucas held his hand out saying, "I sure do. Hear you're expecting your first young'un?"

Shaking Lucas' hand, Chester acknowledged, "Sure am. My wife and I are pretty excited about the whole thing." With that said, Chester turned to the sheriff telling him, "I'll get that warrant and go see the school about those papers."

"Thanks Chester, appreciate you taking care of it." Walking back to his desk, Jonathan sat down motioning for Lucas to do the same.

"What brings you to my neck of the woods? Not on another mission for the Governor, are you?" Johnathan's question had some dread in it as he remembered the last time they were together.

Grinning, Lucas shook his head, "Not this time. I'm no longer with the Governor." Lucas told him.

Frowning, Jonathan asked, "What changed things, if I may ask?"

"Nothing drastic. I was just ready for a change." Lucas replied.

Leaning back in his chair, Jonathan asked, "So what are your plans?"

"Not sure. Been thinking about going home for a spell." Lucas told him.

"You're not rodeo bronc busting anymore?" Jonathan asked.

"Naw, that bullet I took last time I was there kind of put me on the sidelines for a while." Lucas said shrugging his shoulders.

Studying Lucas for a quiet moment, Jonathan sat forward saying, "With Joseph still on his honeymoon, I'm a deputy short. How would you like to fill in for him?"

Lucas fell quiet considering the offer and, as much as he would have liked to accept, he shook his head 'no'. "Like the idea but, Joseph isn't going to be gone more than a few more days then I'd be back in the same spot. Looking for a job."

Jonathan was prepared for Lucas' reasoning so he countered with, "I may be a greenhorn, but I understand training and bronc busting are two different things, am I right?"

Lucas nodded, waiting with a slight feeling of anticipation for the rest of Jonathan's next question, he was sure there was something else coming and he wasn't disappointed.

"I have a shipment of one hundred head of rescued wild Mustangs coming in the next ten days. I need a manager of the J Bar L Ranch. Someone that knows horses, someone that I can trust, someone that can also help as a deputy whenever help is needed. A salary, insurance and, if you like it and want to stay on indefinitely, a partnership in the equine business."

Taking a deep breath, Lucas leaned back, releasing it slowly, "Wow, this is totally unexpected."

Smiling, Jonathan continued with his offer, "There is a small cabin, fully furnished. I've hired two young college guys to work there part time and they would be working with you. You would train them as well as the horses."

"What are your plans concerning these wild mustangs?" Lucas needed to know the answer to that question before he could even consider the offer seriously.

"The hundred consist of twenty pregnant mares, twenty-eight with foals at their side. Ten colts, less than two years old, and the rest are young fillies. The colts and fillies will need to be evaluated to see if they are breeding material or not. Once the mares give birth their foals, they will be evaluated as well as the mares. We want to see if we want to breed them again."

"And what happens to the ones that are seen as not fit to breed?" Lucas asked, holding his breath.

"Well," Jonathan knew full well why Lucas wanted to know the horses' fate. He paused just long enough to make Lucas squirm a little, before telling him. "The J Bar L has twenty-two hundred acres; we can use some as a refuge for those horses. They will have enough timber and hills to roam free, won't have to search for food and have idiots trying to run them down. And with no reproduction it will keep the herd from building, except for the few we might put there."

The grin on Lucas spread from ear to ear and he could hardly restrain himself, "You got yourself a hand Sheriff."

Jonathan's smile broadened as well; he was getting caught up in Lucas' excitement. "You interested in knowing what the plans are for the ones we will work with?" He asked.

Feeling a little sheepish, Lucas nodded saying, "Yeah, I reckon I should know that too."

"The Mustang horse has been a part of America for several hundred years but they are being killed off by the government and the encroaching landowners. The J Bar L is a rescue and preserve for them. We will train them and find homes amongst the growing equestrian sports such as Endurance Riding, Reining, Jumping, and whatever else we find they are capable of learning."

An hour later Jonathan geared down, Lucas leaned back in his chair studying Jonathan for a moment, he asked, "You've been thinking about this a while, haven't you?"

Nodding, Jonathan told him, "Since I was ten years old. Never wanted to be anything but a cop and raise Mustang horses."

"Wasn't much chance of you raising any kind of horse in Chicago, was there?"

"Not hardly, that's what brought me to Texas. No place like Texas when it comes to raising horses. Well, not as far as I'm concerned."

Before Lucas could challenge Jonathan on the horse breeding programs in his home country, the intercom buzzer sounded with Janie announcing Chester's return.

Chester entered with a stack of folders in his arms, smiling at Lucas and the sheriff, he informed them, "Didn't bring all of them, just the ones going back twenty-five years."

Shaking his head, Jonathan wondered out loud, "One small country high school can't have that many employees."

"Yes sir, seems like they did." Chester assured him. Lucas rose to his feet, removing one of the folders from Chester's arms and placed them on the end of Jonathan's desk. Taking one from the top he sat back down and started flipping through the personnel file.

Looking up from the file he was holding, he said, "This could take a little time. I need to go get Sam. She's been stuck in our motel room for about four hours. I'll come back and help go through all of these, once she's had her run."

Standing, Jonathan agreed, "Good idea. Chester will get set up in Joseph's office and you can join him. Mary Wilson is coming by for a visit shortly but once that's done, I'll let you follow me out to the ranch and get you settled in."

"Will do mate," and with a salute toward Chester, Lucas walked out whistling Waltzing Mathilda. Chester turned to Jonathan, asking, "Is Lucas going to work at your ranch?"

"Yeah, figure I needed someone who knows something more about horses than me." Jonathan admitted to him, adding, "He's going to work part time as Deputy until Joseph gets back."

Smiling, Chester nodded his agreement for using Lucas as a deputy. His wife, Vickie, was going to like the fact he might have a little more time off.

## **CHAPTER 2**

For Jonathan, sitting across from Mary Wilson was a revelation. Seeing Mary that morning at the café, he had not realized how drawn and tired she looked. Mary had aged a great deal since her son's arrest.

Trying to keep any pity from showing in his voice, he asked, "How have you been coping, Mary?"

A weak smile was all the answer he needed but she continued on to say, "I'm doing okay Sheriff, I'm sorry, Jonathan."

"It's okay Mary," he said trying to reassure her, "Tell me what's on your mind."

"I need your help," she began, stopping to draw a deep breath, trying to hold back tears. Releasing the deep breath slowly, she continued. "The judge put a restraining order on me when he sent Eric to that facility. He said Eric did not need contact with me for at least six months. I want to see my son, to see with my own eyes he's okay, please help me."

Mary struggled to get her plea spoken without breaking down but with the last word she broke into deep, racking sobs.

Handing Mary a box of tissues, Jonathan remained quiet, giving her the time she needed to regain control. When she finally stopped the heartbreaking sobs, he told her, "I'll speak with the judge but you have to promise me that you'll go see the doctor and have a checkup."

Standing up, he walked around his desk to stand before her. He took her hand and helped her to her feet and added, "You want to feel and look your very best when you go see Eric."

Nodding, Mary tried to smile as she told him, "I'll go, I promise."

"Good, and you tell the doctor's receptionist I said to send me the bill." As Mary started to object, Jonathan softly squeezed her hand, stopping her, "No, that's the condition, no exception."

This time Mary managed a small smile, saying, "You are a good friend Jonathan, thank you."

Walking her to the door, Jonathan reassured her, "Everything will work out. Stay strong."

Nodding, Mary promised, "I will, and I won't forget this."

Walking out of his office with her, Jonathan stood and watched as she walked out into the parking lot before he crossed over to Janie's desk.

"Janie, call Judge Bosshart's office and see if he has a little time for me tomorrow morning. Let him know I'll bring coffee and donuts."

"Yes sir," Janie paused for a second before hesitantly asking, "Sheriff, is Lucas Wilson going to be working with us from here on?"

"Looks that way, why do you ask?"

"No reason, really," Janie answered but then smiling really big, she added, "Other than he is a cutie. He married or otherwise taken?"

Laughing, Jonathan shook his head saying, "He is not taken in any way but you might want to go slow. Lucas has a wandering foot, need to see how long he's going to be around."

Giving Jonathan a shy grin Janie said, "Maybe if he gets to know me, he will want to stick around."

"I hope he will." Turning to go join Chester in the squad room he stopped, turned back to Janie and asked, "You're a pretty good equestrian, aren't you?"

Nodding, Janie proclaimed, "Yes Sir, two-time winner in the NRA Barrel Racing for Harris County Rodeo competition."

"How would you like to help me out with a program I'm starting out at my ranch?" Before she could answer he added, "You'd be working with Lucas."

Janie's smile lit her face as she told him, "Count me in."

"Good, we can talk tomorrow after I meet with the Judge. You'd start after Lillian gets back." His cell phone ringing stopped any further conversation. Jonathan checked the name of the incoming caller; it wasn't one he recognized. His "Sheriff Lawrence" was met by a male voice on the other end.

"Sheriff my name is Peter James and I need to meet with you about the dead man on the school grounds."

"I'm in my office, how about right now?" Jonathan replied.

James released a sigh saying, "I'm in your parking lot. I would like not to be seen."

Peter James was scared of that, Jonathan was sure. He told him, "Drive around to the back of the courthouse I'll meet you at the back entrance."

Less than three minutes later Jonathan let Peter James in the back door. Jonathan led him to his office through his private entrance without speaking. James appeared to be in his sixties, around five feet ten, slightly overweight with a midlife spread with a crop of snow-white hair and blue eyes. In his office Jonathan gestured for James to sit in the chair opposite his desk.

Jonathan was certain he had heard a slight accent when James had talked on the phone a few minutes before and his old familiar itch of caution crawled up his spine once again.

"You seem to be to be under a great deal of stress Mr. James. What knowledge do you have about my DOA?" Jonathan asked.

"His name is Henri Gustaf, he is from Russia, as I am. He was here to meet with me. I did not kill Comrade Gustaf." James stated in a hurried tone.

If Jonathan was surprised by James' announcement, he gave no indication as James continued.

"I met with Gustaf and we talked. He understood my reluctance to go back to Russia to live. I have lived here in America nearly all my life. My children are here, my wife is buried here, she was an American." James' voice cracked ever so slightly but he managed to continue while Jonathan sat quietly listening.

"Gustaf said he would give me time to talk to my children. To plan what I would do. If I went back, my children would be left alone by Russian officials or they could choose to go with me."

"And would your children be going with you? Jonathan interrupted to ask.

James' smile was sad, "My sons are successful adults, one is married and has two beautiful children. My eldest, Christopher, is an attorney with a very large firm in Houston. The other, Charles, he is single. He is a children's doctor at the Children's hospital in Galveston. They will not wish to disrupt their lives by moving to Russia."

Jonathan interrupted again to ask, "When did you talk to Gustaf?

"This morning at the school. I am the Maintenance Superintendent." James answered, adding, "We met on the roof, where we were less likely to be seen."

"Why are you talking to me now Mr. James?" was something Jonathan really wanted to know.

"Because I will be killed next." James' answer was not what Jonathan had expected.

"What makes you believe that?" Jonathan asked.

"Because Gustaf told me there were ten of us brought here to America but, when he was given the list, there were eleven names on it. There is one here that Gustaf was not the contact for."

The more James talked, the more apparent it became that he was very frightened.

"Were you told this eleventh man's name?" Jonathan asked, hoping that he would be lucky enough this time to get some good news.

"Gustaf said he was registered with the KGB as Andre Jenkins but Gustaf did not know if Comrade Jenkins was his real name." James answered adding, "Supposedly, Comrade Jenkins is an engineer. He was trained in Moscow."

"Did Gustaf happen to show you a picture of this Andre fellow?" Jonathan asked.

Nodding James tells him, "Yes but, he was very young, maybe twenty or so."

"If you sit down in front of a sketch artist you think you could describe what the guy looked like?" Jonathan asked.

Jonathan's relief was evident as James told him, "I think I can, I will certainly try."

Picking up his desk phone, he told Janie to get a hold of the police sketch artist and tell him he needs him for a sketch, ASAP. Redirecting his attention back to Peter James, Jonathan studies him for a few moments before asking, "What did your sons have to say when you told them who you were? When did you tell them?"

"My eldest, Christopher, was really upset. He does not like the idea of me going back to Moscow. I told him I wanted to but only for a visit. I had left family back there and good friends. I want to see them again before I die. I spoke to my eldest a couple of hours ago." James shook his head saying. "My son, he is an attorney, he worries too much about me but he finally understood."

With a warm smile he continued, "My youngest, his name is Charles, I spoke on the phone to him only minutes before I heard of Gustaf's' death. He said he is packing and going with me." Seeing the surprise on the Sheriff's face, he quickly added, "Not to stay forever you understand but he wants to visit the children's hospitals and talk with Russian doctors. Russia has very good medical laboratories he wants to visit, like Doctors Across Borders."

Nodding, Jonathan did understand why the young Charles James would want to go. But one thing was still unclear. "What was the mission if you had been activated?"

None too proud of what he was about to say, James sighed answering, "Your refineries, destroy them or as many as we could. Close your waterfront. Disrupt and destroy as much of your oil flow as we could."

"So, you and the others were planted in, around, and near all of our refineries here in the States?" Jonathan asked, almost in disbelief.

James was not surprised at the slight sound of disbelief in the Sheriff's voice, there were times he had been flooded with the same feeling.

"The accepted thought of our leaders at the time was if your oil industry was hit hard your attention would be upon the recouping and repairing of your refineries. Our military would take that confusion and strike at the heart of your country." James told him, the tone of his voice rising. The plan had been so simple and so very, very much ideal.

A soft knock on the door announced the arrival of a uniformed deputy, Jason Allen. He entered armed with several pencils and sketch pad. The introduction to James did not include the details as to why the sketch was needed. Thirty minutes later the drawing was complete and given to Jonathan. The drawing showed a young face, a head full of raven black hair and sky-blue eyes. There was nothing distinctive about the face except for one identifying mark on the left jaw. A birthmark, tan in color and in the unmistakable shape of a lightning bolt.

Handing the sketch back to the deputy, Jonathan asked, "Can you computer-age this? The guy would be in his late sixties. Do one with a beard and one without."

Deputy Allen nodded, "Yes sir, shouldn't take more than half an hour."

"Great, get Janie to make copies for you and the other deputies. I want each to carry the sketch on a clipboard. This guy might not be living here but he's looking for Mr. James, he just might be walking our streets. I want him picked up. Tell Chester to come in on your way out."

Nodding Deputy Allen scurried off to do as Jonathan instructed. Waiting until the door closed, Jonathan turned back to James saying, "Mr. James, we need to see about getting you to a safe house. It's obvious you cannot stay in your home."

Peter James started to object but held it back as Chester entered the sheriff's office. He also understood that to remain in his home would put a target on his back. He said hesitantly, "There are some things I will need."

Nodding Jonathan told him, "I will have two deputies stay with you while you pack up. You understand you cannot tell anyone where you are, that includes your sons, not until this Andre Jenkins is caught. No one, is that understood?"

James nodded his understanding but made one last plea, "May I call my sons to tell them I won't be talking to them for a while, not until it is safe?"

"You can do that while I'm arranging for your transport and safe house." Jonathan told him. Walking toward his office door, he stopped, and turning back to James, he told him, "You will leave your cell phone here."

James, eyes sad and shoulders slumped with weariness spoke, "This is not how I visualized my senior years."

Jonathan nodded and walked out of the door without making a reply. He couldn't think of a reply, hell's bells the guy was a Russian agent. He didn't have time to feel sorry for him.

Turning to Chester he instructed, "Take two deputies and have them stay with James while he is getting his belongings, they are to stay until they are relieved. You follow them make sure they are settled in."

A sharp "Yes sir," and Chester went out of the courthouse front entrance, almost bumping into the county district attorney. Zachery Golightly was of a small stature, standing five foot six inches, his light brown hair was thinning on top which made the thin straight-line mustache and neatly trimmed salt and pepper beard even more noticeable.

Jonathan's soft spoken "Hell" came as a response to Golightly's sappy wave, he didn't want to converse with Golightly.

Golightly stopped in front of Jonathan saying, "That young deputy was acting like a fire has been set under him."

Ignoring Golightly's assessment of Chester's speed, Jonathan tried not to show his annoyance, instead he asked,

"What can I do for you Mr. Golightly?"

Golightly glanced around checking the closeness of any eavesdroppers before saying, "Sheriff, I realize you and your officer are working hard to quickly settle this awful thing that happened at our high school."

Jonathan tried to pay attention to what Golightly said but was distracted by the small thin mustache that bobbed up and down on the district attorney's upper lip.

Jonathan jolted back to attention with Golightly's question, "Sheriff, the parents are concerned about sending their kids back to our high school if this awful mess isn't taken care of soon. Do you have an identity for the deceased? Or have any idea who might have done this terrible deed?"

"There is nothing that I can release at this time." Before Golightly could ask any more questions, Jonathan added, "There will be a statement released tomorrow to bring the public up to date."

Seeing a tall, well-dressed black man enter the courthouse, Jonathan excused himself "Mr. Golightly you'll have to excuse me I have someone I need to talk to."

Jonathan walked quickly toward Sheridan, not giving Golightly any chance for another question. Recognizing the irritation on Jonathan's face, FBI Agent, Phillip Sheridan opened his mouth to inquire what was up. Jonathan's "To the morgue" said through gritted teeth cut him off.

Falling in beside the sheriff, Sheridan brought him up to date, "Gustaf, from what I can gather is, was, a top-notch agent. He never failed to carry out an assignment and they were always clean and professional. He has been retired for the past ten years but still has the ear of top Russian government bureaucrats."

"If he was such a professionally clean fellow, how come he left a string of dead guys wherever he went?" Jonathan asked but before Sheridan could answer he said, "Gustaf didn't kill them, Jenkins did."

"That's what we figure and with Gustaf dead, it kind of confirms it."

"So, what are your next steps?" Jonathan asked, hoping there was a next step.

A shake of his head and Sheridan's lop-sided grin served as an answer, Jonathan knew his FBI buddy didn't have a clue but that wouldn't keep him from giving an opinion.

"Well it seems to me you have the next step since you got this tenth mole stashed in a safe house with guards, I'd say you've got a snake by the tail."

Jonathan really did not need Sheridan to tell him that. Ignoring it, Jonathan pressed forward with his next question, "The thing is, how long will Jenkins hang around waiting for his chance?"

Jonathan didn't wait for Sheridan's reply before adding, "We have to do something to bring Jenkins out. Keeping James hidden isn't going to do it but setting James up as bait just might."

Surprise at Jonathan's disregard for the safety of a fellow human was evident on Sheridan's face. Reading the shocked look Jonathan snapped, "Hell Phil, I don't intend to stake the guy out on an ant hill."

"Glad to hear that but just what are you thinking?" Sheridan's question was apprehensive.

"Off the top of my head I'd say we need to hold a press conference. Our citizens are wanting to know about the dead guy found on our school grounds." Pausing briefly for effect Jonathan continued, "So let's give them the facts. I'll talk to Sam tonight, have her call her editor at the Chronicle. We'll get the newspapers as well as the television stations."

"And then what?" Sheridan asked. Not waiting for an answer, he added, "You think this killer is gonna make a try for James at the press conference? Where are you going to hold this press conference? On the courthouse steps?"

"Exactly." was the answer Jonathan gave him. "We don't know why Jenkins is killing the ten, but we do know that is what he is doing. I want him alive and I want answers."

"Alright, set your conference up. I'll get some extra men to help keep it from turning into a blood bath." Sheridan felt less than excited about Jonathan's plan, but he also knew that there would be no stopping Jonathan beyond locking him up.

That night on the phone with his bride, Jonathan braced himself for Samantha's reaction when he told her about James and the press conference.

"Are you trying to get yourself killed?" was about what he expected.

"Your friend Sheridan and I have a bet as to what would be your first remark," Jonathan was trying not to laugh as he added, "I won."

"Ha, ha, very funny Lawrence." Samantha's snarl was good-natured as she changed the subject. "I'm winding things up here in Austin tomorrow."

"That means you are coming home?" his question had a touch of excitement in it.

"Yes, I'm coming in tomorrow by noon. I heard from Lillian; they will be home by tomorrow as well."

Frowning, Jonathan asked, "They're cutting their honeymoon short, why?"

Samantha wasn't sure if she should answer truthfully or tell a little white lie. She decided on a half-truth.

"Because I have called a meeting with the four of us and you'd do just as well to not ask me why because I will not say. But it is something the four of us need to talk about and decide upon."

For a few moments Jonathan went silent as his brain ran amuck trying to figure out just what it might be that had put a burr under Samantha. Knowing it would do little good to try and persuade her to talk beforehand and knowing what he was facing at the present, he let it go saying, "Alright, just remember you are going to owe me big time."

Laughing Samantha agreed, "I will remember," her last softly spoken words were "I love you."

Hanging up his phone Jonathan knew whatever it was Samantha was keeping from him would have to wait but a growing knot of apprehension was tingling up his spine.

SUE LAND

Shaking his new partner's hand, Jonathan told him, "It will do, considering all the work and time you will be putting in to get things up and running."

Turning with his back to the fence, Lucas hooked a boot heel over the bottom railing asking, "When did you say the first group of mares were due in?"

"You've got two weeks to get yourself settled in. That enough time?"

As Sam came bounding toward them Lucas laughed, answering, "Yeah, I say it's more than enough. Sam already seems settled in."

"Ok, then I will leave you and Sam to get acquainted with everything. We can talk tonight when I come in. You see anything that needs changing just have at it."

Walking with Jonathan back to his car, Lucas changed the subject back to one he knew was eating at the Sheriff.

"I was talking to Chester and he told me about the press conference. When do you plan on giving it?" he asked.

Jonathan took a deep breath, blowing out his answer, "This afternoon."

The answer surprised Lucas a little, "You think the killer is going to be forced to show his hand?"

"Yeah," Jonathan said, wishing he was as sure as he sounded. "The longer our perp waits, the more chances he's taking at being identified. And the greater the odds are he will kill again to protect that identity."

The drive back to his office was uneventful and gave Jonathan time to rethink the happenings of the past week. Being a small-town sheriff was not anything he had expected, for one thing it was most assuredly a small town. City politics took front row and the infighting was just as corrupt and vicious as any big city politics. Everyone knew everyone. They were either blood relatives or married into the family. There was always a top-dog, the one everyone listened to and followed the lead of on any city agenda. You would think the top-dog would be the Mayor since that was the highest elected office. But, not their mayor, he was a follower. That was how he got elected, by following the top-dog's advice. Someone that wanted to be elected to more than one term did not dare to have an agenda that wasn't approved by the top-dog. Jonathan had long suspected the head of Kullpepper Construction Company, Christopher Kullpepper was the top-dog. It was no secret that he had his finger in every large construction job taking place in and around Liberty. From the newest hotel to the new nursing facility. It also was no secret that members of the city council met for coffee and cigars at Kullpepper's office every morning and most assuredly the night before any city council meeting was to convene. Jonathan knew he needed someone to turn on Kullpepper and testify to what discussions and agreements were reached in the pre-council meeting before he could call in the State Attorney.

Jonathan's thoughts were depressing him, so when his cell phone rang, he answered, relieved. "Lawrence."

Janie's voice replied "Sheriff, Chester just called in a deputy down, out on Route 314 near the dam."

"Hell! Let him know I'm on my way." Jonathan instructed as he switched on his lights and siren.

Fifteen minutes later Jonathan parked his jeep met by Chester.

"What happened?" Jonathan asked as the two walked to the ambulance's back door where the medics were tending Deputy Mark Winslow. Keeping up with Jonathan's long strides, Chester quickly told him, "It's not clear, there's no one close by that could see or hear anyone. What was he doing out here on this county road? We have a lot of questions but no answers. He put in a call to the station by Deputy Winslow to time out for coffee."

"You go to the hospital and stay with Deputy Winslow, no one gets in to see him besides me. Understood?"

Chester's "Yes sir!" was said as he spun on his heels and ran back to his squad car to fall in behind the ambulance as it pulled away.

Looking at the pool of blood on the roadside, Jonathan realizes his slow, small town life was no longer slow and that was something he did not like. The world was seemingly going to hell in a handbasket from where he stood. Motioning to the crime scene photographer, Trent Bistro, he told him to cover the entire road and all surrounding grounds. Getting in his car, he turned around and drove back to his office.

Janie was waiting to hand him three slips of paper with messages, all for return calls. Sitting at his desk, the first call was Sheridan's.

"Your fellow still willing to give a statement to the press?" was Sheridan's opening question.

A little surprised, Jonathan's answer was short, "Yeah, why?"

"Well hell man, you keep getting your citizens shot. I sure as hell wouldn't want to be your Judas goat."

Sheridan replied, trying not to laugh, but he knew he had just kicked a sleeping dog. Sure, enough Jonathan's reply left him without a doubt.

"And you can go to hell Sheridan." Jonathan said in a heated snarl.

Laughing, Sheridan tried to smooth over his poor joke, "Sorry pal, thought you'd be in a better frame of mind seeing as how your bride is coming home."

Jonathan switched thoughts, asking, "How did you know Sam's coming home? You have eyes on me?"

"Hell no, my wife called to check on yours last evening. You think somebody's got eyes on you?"

"Damned if I know. This embedded KGB thing could go deep. Why are the sleepers being killed? Are they all refusing to go home quietly?"

"Those are questions we need to answer. Putting yours out there as a sitting duck could backfire. Whoever this perp is, he seems to know what he is doing." Was Sheridan's only help, and it wasn't one Johnathan took lightly.

"Have you been able to back track Gustaf? Other than the dead bodies left in his wake?" Johnathan asked.

"No, the killings were all clean, with exception of Gustaf." Was the answer coming from Sheridan.

Slowly, Jonathan voiced a thought that had been nagging him for the past few hours. "What if this isn't about the Sleepers? What if there is something deeper? Russia is not to be trusted; we all know that. Yet we, like lambs to the slaughter, took their word that Gustaf was sent here to retract embedded KGB sleepers?"

There was a moment of silence before Sheridan asked, "What are you thinking?"

Jonathan followed Sheridan's question with an admission. "I've absolutely no reason to think it, but supposing the perp isn't carrying out orders to eliminate those that refuse to leave but just eliminate them period. Putin doesn't need the crazies in Washington screaming even louder for his scalp. So, he sends Gustaf to find them and the assassin to eliminate them. Gustaf faces the assassin and he's eliminated."

"Complicated web to be sure," Sheridan said before asking, "but why would Putin want them killed? Having them sent back to Russia is a lot quieter than leaving dead bodies in your wake."

"Yeah," Jonathan agreed but the idea was not letting go, "Unless our assassin isn't working for the Russian government."

It was silent for a moment until Sheridan exclaimed exasperatedly, "Aw hell!"

"And I hit a nerve, damnit Sheridan what the Hell are you keeping from me?" Jonathan demanded.

"I'm twenty minutes away." Sheridan's short reply was followed by a click. Jonathan resisted the urge to throw his phone and instead slammed the palm of his hand down hard on the steering wheel.

## **CHAPTER 4**

The quiet was tense as Jonathan waited for Sheridan to finish their conversation. Jonathan wanted the day to be over, he wanted the damn Gustaf thing to be over. All he wanted was to be sleeping in the warm arms of his bride. He braced himself for what was to come as Sheridan dropped the other shoe.

"I reckon you are not naive enough not to know that the U.S. conducts espionage in other nations and they on us. Ours is done under the National Clandestine Service. Britain's are controlled by the Secret Intelligence Service.

In the 20's the Russians focus was mainly on our military and industrial complexes, especially the aircraft and munitions industries and penetrating our federal government bureaucracies like the US Department of State and the War Department. The US had no idea how deep the Russians had gotten, not until Francis Gary Powers U2 was shot down in 1960. They had gotten their hands on the radio beacon artillery fuses developed during WWII. Our counterpart, Britain's SIS let us know that we needed to do another sweep. Seems like our closet has not been completely cleaned out. They say there is still one lone rat dropping pellets and gnawing his way to our national secrets. Now, is this one lone wolf the one who is doing all the killings? I don't believe he is but then I don't run the FBI, CIA, or the Secret Service. I'm just a lone agent, on disability, howling in the wind into deaf ears."

Leaning back in his chair, Jonathan sat quietly, digesting what Sheridan had just told him. Several minutes passed before he sat forward, shaking his head, voicing his response.

"Our bodies are middle aged, forgotten plants, totally guilty of nothing but being in the states illegally. Their families are normal average citizens, the most any of them are guilty of is skipping school. The Feds, NCS, or whatever you want to call it, may have a plant still to weed out of their playhouse but that's not our scenario."

Sheridan was slow to respond, digesting what Jonathan had just said.

"Okay, so who and what, is behind this string of killings, where the victims just happen to be Russian spies?" Sheridan inquired with a touch of mockery.

Jonathan did not miss the tone but chose to ignore it, "Someone who has the means to hire a professional to get rid of the embedded spies by following Gustaf around. Someone who does not want it known that he is the offspring of one of those spies which could mean a financial or personal disaster. A personal embarrassment that could ruin him or her."

Before Sheridan could respond, Jonathan continued, "Right now, I've got a deputy in the hospital fighting for his life. Do I think he is part of this? I sure as hell do, I do not believe in coincidences."

Nodding, Sheridan tended to agree with Jonathan but he still had one more question, "And what about James? You're sticking him out there like a sitting duck, giving your shooter a chance to blow the guy's head off."

The expression on Jonathan's face was all the answer Sheridan needed. Getting to his feet, he said, "Alright, let me make a call and I'll get you that help I promised."

Walking Sheridan to the door, Johnathan told him, "The press release will be at four this afternoon on the steps of the courthouse. I'll have six deputies that I trust as James' personal guards and twelve State troopers cover the courthouse grounds. If your guys can mingle with the press?"

Nodding, Sheridan assured Jonathan, "My guys, five of them will be there, I know each of them personally."

Grinning at him, Jonathan said, "Be sure your guys introduce themselves to mine, don't want one of them to get shot by mistake."

Sheridan knew his friend was only half-joking but he would make sure the good guys were acquainted with each other.

As Sheridan walked out, Jonathan's phone sounded off. Glancing at the caller ID, Jonathan answered saying, "Sam, you're home?"

His wife's soft laugh tingles his spine as she assured him that she is indeed home, "Got here about twenty minutes ago. Can you come by and say good morning?"

Laughing Jonathan told her, "Like to see someone try and stop me."

In five seconds, Jonathan was out of his office door, yelling to Janie that he would be back in an hour or so. Never had he thought about the drive from the courthouse to his ranch being long, but it seemed endless now. Soon enough though, he entered through the front door of his house, sweeping Samantha up in his arms, carrying her to the bedroom whispering, "I'm home too."

## CHAPTER 5

Sitting at the kitchen table, nursing a tepid cup of coffee, Jonathan brought his thoughts back to the case.

"As glorious as you are and resisting the temptation to take you back to bed, I need you to get into your reporter rags and work for me. Get a press crowd here on the courthouse by four this afternoon. Think you can get the T.V. out as well as print?"

Nodding, Samantha's brows are pulled together in a deep frown as she asks, "Just what are you planning?"

Jonathan wasn't sure how to put into words his plan but he answered Samantha's question, "I want to see who shows up for the press conference. Maybe our killer will make a try before the conference, or at the conference. We will say that in two days James is going before the DOJ and will spill his guts. He was a witness to the Gustaf killing and he can identify the killer. But, only after the DOJ gives him a deal."

"You have James hidden from the world, how are you going to give your killer a chance to try for him? Why two days?" Samantha asked.

"Two days for the plea deal to be written up. Setting him up as a decoy is the one way to catch the killer." Was the short answer Jonathan gave, adding, "Details will be worked out."

Knowing the question Samantha was about to ask Jonathan told her, "I promise I won't get shot."

Samantha fell quiet for several minutes. She wanted to rant and rave at her husband but realizing it would do little good, she gave a short nod of acceptance and left to get dressed.

Picking up his cell phone, which had been lying next to his now cold cup of coffee, Jonathan pushed his office number. When Janie answered, he instructed, "Get a hold of Chester, tell him to meet me at my office in forty-five minutes."

"Yes sir. And Sheriff, the report came back on the ballistics from the bullet from Deputy Winslow. It was from the same gun that killed the man at the school."

## CHAPTER 3

Coffee with Judge Phillip Bosshart the next morning did not prove to be as tough a job as Jonathan had anticipated. The Judge agreed to let Mary have a short visit with her son in two weeks. With the understanding that there would be no other visits until the doctors all agreed upon what effect she had had on the boy.

Talking to Mary on the phone proved to be harder since Mary could not understand why she had to wait another two weeks. It took a few minutes of calming her down for her to finally accept the stipulations. It was the Judge's way or no visit at all for another six months, and so, reluctantly she agreed.

Walking into the courthouse, Johnathan found he was able to smile again as a beautiful gray and white German shepherd dog came bounding across the lobby to greet him. Going down on his knees, he hugged the joyful dog, laughing and trying to avoid as many of her kisses as he could. When the dog finally figured she had had enough of the hugs and kisses, Jonathan got to his feet and greeted Lucas Wilson, "You two must have gotten up early this morning."

Grinning, Lucas shook his head saying, "Yeah, I made a mistake last night telling Sam we were going to our new home."

Looking down at Sam who seemed to be watching and understood that the two men were talking about her, she happily allowed Jonathan to reach down and scratch her ear.

"The ol' girl just doesn't like the city." was his comment. Straightening back up he said, "So let's take her and show her the new home. See what she thinks."

Half of an hour later Johnathan and Lucas stood leaning on the coral fence as Sam checked out the barn and pens.

Glancing off across the green fields and scanning the timberline that ran toward the distant hills, a sigh escaped Lucas, "I think Sam and I are home." Turning to Jonathan he held his hand out, "Saying thank you does not seem adequate for the opportunity you are giving me."

Jonathan was not surprised to hear there was a connection, mainly because the case was a screwed-up jigsaw puzzle from the get-go. Telling Janie thanks, he stood up and walked out of the back door. Remembering his last words to Samantha, he could only wish he felt as confident as he had tried to make Samantha believe he was.

Back at his office, Chester was waiting and after hearing Jonathan's new instructions he was not sure he understood, so with some apprehension he questioned, "And, I am to video the news conference looking for what exactly? How am I to cover the parking lot and street entirely?"

Smiling at Chester's doubts, Johnathan repeated, telling him, "I want you to video the reporters and whoever else shows up for the press release. I want to see what each expression is like, their movements, and anything else that looks remotely unsuitable or out of place. I want their reactions, I want their surprise, their shock, their anger, whatever. You obviously cannot video the entire lot and street so concentrate on those up front and the reporters. Chester, give me something to look at."

Nodding, Chester took a deep breath, releasing it slowly he agreed, "Alright Sheriff, I will get you all the footage I can with the one camera. But thinking about it we might be better served if there is a second camera shooting at the same time? Coming in from the opposite side."

Jonathan agreed, "Yeah, I do too but I haven't found a second camera man available with such short notice. You know someone we could get at the last minute?"

Chester jumped to his feet saying, "Yeah sir, I'll give him a call and let you know what he says."

As Chester ran out, Jonathan shouted after him, "Have him come in, now!" Chester gave him the thumbs up, shutting the sheriff's office door behind him.

Jonathan leaned back in his chair, breathing deep. He was sure he was on the right track but something was still eating at him. He had learned long ago to follow his gut, and right then his gut was dining on his backbone.

Less than an hour later, Chester came back and making introductions between Jonathan and his childhood buddy, Martin Sanchez. Sanchez had black hair, black eyes, a dark complexion and had a muscular yet slender six-foot frame.

The most pivotal point with Sanchez's appearance, as far as Jonathan was concerned, was the nose-ring. Shaking hands with the young cameraman, Jonathan chose to ignore it for the time being.

"Let's walk outside so I can show you guys what I have in mind for the shoot."

Leading the way out, Jonathan did not miss the big smile and thumbs up that Chester gave his friend.

It took only a few minutes for Sanchez to impress Jonathan with his camera talent. Technically, Sanchez was sharp and had a good working knowledge of angles and for the equipment as well as a full understanding of what Jonathan wanted.

Smiling, Sanchez repeated Jonathan's attempt at camera instructions.

"Gotcha Sheriff, the crowd, closeup on each face, clear and sharp for easy recognition. Chester will shoot from your left shoulder to the middle of the parking lot. I will shoot from your right shoulder meeting Chester in the middle. We both will do breakaways to catch any passing automobile's plate numbers. Chester will take the north bound, I will handle the south bound." Finishing with the details, Sanchez gave him a big grin asking, "That about cover it, Sheriff?"

Jonathan stood studying Sanchez for several minutes before nodding and telling him, "Lose the nose ring" as he turned and walked back into the courthouse.

Walking back to his office, Jonathan motioned for Janie to follow him. Sitting down at his desk, he was quiet for a moment before telling her, "Get a hold of Lucas, tell him he needs to go pick up our witness, bring him in the back way here at the courthouse. We need to prepare our guy for his press debut."

Nodding, Janie turned to leave but stopped and turned back saying, "Sheriff, a Kenneth Gessner called a few moments ago, he said to tell you that the flood gates at the Trinity will be opened at noon."

"Damn," was muttered as Jonathan turned and headed back outside, telling Janie over his shoulder, "I'll get the Federal Emergency Management alerted to look at the old Snake River Estates, you notify the schools they need to release, now."

Jonathan did not wait for a reply from Janie. He knew that being raised in these parts, she was aware of the steps people living in and around the Trinity River took to prepare for possible flooding. The rain had stopped during the night but she knew as well as Jonathan that the drain off was still occurring and the ditches and creeks were beyond capacity.

Releasing his cell phone from his belt and placing it on speaker, Jonathan punched the F.E.N.'s and had William "Bill" Robertson's personal number in. When Robertson answered, he wasted no time filling him in on the floodgate and the press conference telling Robertson, "I need your guys to keep an eye on the bridge out on county road 214, Tex-Dot will be closing it off but it's looking shaky."

"Thanks, I'll send a couple of guys out to see if they can take a reading." Robertson assured him but added, "What's this I hear about you got the guy that did the killing at the school?"

"Damn! News sure does travel fast in a small town. The truth is no." Jonathan answered Robertson, telling him, "Not the guy but someone who might have seen something. We will know more when I get him in the office, Deputy Wilson is bringing him in."

William Robertson was in his mid-sixties, tall, slim, and white-haired with a neatly trimmed white beard. Born and raised in Liberty and the surrounding counties, Robertson had no reservation in asking the sheriff anything he felt he had the right to know and right now he wanted to know who the witness was.

"I am hearing talk Sheriff, about who this witness you have is, and he might not be as reliable as you think." Robertson informed Jonathan with just a touch of arrogance in his voice.

Jonathan was familiar with the tone that Robertson used when he was trying to impress with his knowledge and or position. Right then, Jonathan didn't know what it was Robertson was trying to convey but he did want to know from where and from whom Robertson was getting his information.

"Commissioner, rumors fly really fast in small towns, but you seem to have knowledge that is a little above normal gossip. Just how do you know my witness might not be reliable?" Jonathan inquired, his nerves tightening.

Robertson hesitated a few seconds before finally disclosing, "Hell, Lawrence half the town knows you've got Peter James, our High School maintenance guy, in protective custody. Old James, he's been known to tell a wild tale or two, most of them made up fantasies."

Unsure if he should encourage Robertson, Jonathan took his chances by asking, "What kind of wild tales?"

"Well, the only one I really know is the one my sister's kid came home telling. James was supposed to be a government spy for a foreign country during the 'Nam conflict."

"'Nam?" Jonathan's voice regaled all the absurdity of the statement.

"Yeah, 'Nam," Robertson said laughing at the absurdity of it as well, "The old coot is most likely crazier than a loon."

James certainly had not sounded loony, nor had his story been unbelievable, especially with what they knew about him. Jonathan did not want to hear anything further from Robertson, so he cut him short, "Be sure and have your guys check that bridge out and let me know what they find."

Jonathan did not wait for a reply from Robertson. Hanging up, he felt that old familiar itch crawling up his spine. *"Hell, what am I missing?"* Whatever it was, he sure as hell was going to find out. Removing his cell phone from his belt, he dialed the Galveston Sheriff's direct number. When Sheriff Jerome Hanson's voice broadcast his thick southern "Sheriff Hanson", Jonathan wasted no time letting the sheriff know why he was calling.

"Jerome, it's Jonathan Lawrence, need your help."

"Hell Jonathan, only time you ever call is when you need my help. So, what is it this time?"

"I got a couple of names, like for you to see what you can come up with... A Christopher James, Attorney and Charles James a children's doctor there in Galveston."

"And just what might you be looking for, my friend?"

Jerome Hanson was no fool and was not to be taken lightly. The man was a hard-nosed cop and did not take lightly to someone treading on his boundaries, so Jonathan was quick to let him know that this was not the case.

"We have a guy here we are holding as a potential witness to a murder, name's Peter James our High School Caretaker. These two are his sons, want to know a little about them."

"Murder, huh?" was the only reply Hanson offered but Jonathan understood him well enough to know the Sheriff had accepted the short version. What he was about to add would most likely put a burr under Hanson's saddle as he told him, "Jerome, I need what you can get, like in the next couple of hours."

"Damn, what's the hurry?" Jerome roared.

"Holding a press conference, I want to be sure of James' story and his background before I go out on a limb."

"Yeah, I can see that. Okay, will see what I can do."

Before Jonathan can express a word of thanks, Hanson hung up. Clipping his cell phone back on his belt, Jonathan smiled. He had known Hanson for the past fifteen years. They worked together on several cases that connected the two counties. The hard-nosed jackass had not changed one little bit but there wasn't a better guy to have protecting your back than Sheriff Jerome Hanson.

Janie barged through his door shouting, "Lucas is being shot at!"

Leaping to his feet, Jonathan followed Janie out the door questioning, "Where is he?"

"He's at the safe house! Sheriff, Lucas says Mr. James is shot."

"Get an ambulance out there." He yelled, running toward the exit. "And get a couple of other units out there."

Following after him, Janie yelled back, "Chester and one other squad car are already on their way."

Janie's last words were yelled as Jonathan slammed his jeep door and in seconds, he spun out of the courthouse parking lot.

Exactly ten minutes later, Jonathan pulled into the driveway of the safe house where Lucas was waiting. Getting out of his jeep, frustration and anger overloaded, as he demanded to know.

"What the hell happened?"

Walking around the jeep, Lucas understood Jonathan's anger, he was beginning to feel explosive himself.

"I no more than drive up when James opens the front door and walks out followed by two deputies. About two seconds later this dark blue four-door Chevy barrels down the opposite side of the street and opens fire. The shooter sprays about six rounds before turning the corner. When the shooting is over, James is down, a minor wound in his left shoulder. He's on the way to the ER with the two deputies as guards."

"Did you get a look at the driver? Or get the car plate numbers?"

Shaking his head Lucas said, "My back was to the car when the shooting started. I dropped down, using my car as a shield. By the time I turned to fire back the car was turning the corner."

"How the hell did the shooter know James was here?"

Lucas wished he had an answer for the Sheriff but that was not the only question for which he wanted answers.

"The six rounds were fired in an arc, they landed in the front of the house, above the door, through the window on the right side of the door, above the window, the fifth hit James, and we haven't found the sixth round."

Walking to the front door, Jonathan turned back to face Lucas saying, "This smells like my grandpa's outhouse."

Unable to hold a lopsided grin from spreading across his lips, Lucas nodded saying, "Growing up as a kid my outhouse was the entire outback."

The seriousness of the situation erased his grin almost instantly as he said, "Something definitely smells about this whole thing."

Walking back to his vehicle Jonathan climbed in, turned the ignition and told Lucas, "Stay here until the CSI guys arrive. I want the parking spot of our shooter swept for every grain of dirt." Backing out, he raised his voice in anger, "and find me those slugs!"

## CHAPTER 6

Entering the Livingston County Hospital, it didn't take a genius to know something wrong had just happened. The speakers were blasting for people to remain in place and the doors on the emergency room were locked down as well as the elevators.

The hospital security guard spotted the Sheriff as he entered and started a quick jog toward Jonathan who stopped and waited for him.

The tag on his shirt pocket identified Sergeant Winston Miller, a large framed gentleman who moved lightly on his feet. Jonathan figured the Sergeant was near sixty, had very few grays scattered amongst his raven black head of hair, and his gray eyes were bright and clear, no glasses or contacts. To top it off, the guy was not even breathless from his jog over. Jonathan did not wait for the guard to speak, demanding, "What the hell is going on?"

"I was just notified they have a missing patient on third floor Sheriff, one that your guys brought in."

"Aw hell!"

Jonathan did not wait for the Sergeant, he took off at a dead run toward the elevators, snapping at the guard to, "Activate the damn elevator."

The few seconds it took to arrive on the third floor seemed like minutes. Deputy Wayne Hendricks was waiting for him.

"What the hell happened Hendricks?" Jonathan asked.

"Deputy Rollins and I were on guard at James' door in the hall. I had to empty my bladder." Shaking his head, Hendricks was clearly shaken, "Hell Sheriff, I couldn't have been gone more than three minutes. I came back, and Rollins is nowhere to be seen in the hall, so I enter the room. Rollins is laying on the floor and James' bed is empty."

Wayne Hendricks has been a Deputy for Jonathan for a little over two years, he was young, just twenty-two but he had always proven to be reliable and could be counted on to do his job, so taking a deep breath Jonathan eased up, asking, "How's Rollins?"

Jake Rollins was a different story, a policeman for over twenty years, both in big cities as well as small towns. He had to have been taken by surprise to have lost his perp.

"Doc says he's some confused and he has a king-sized goose egg on his noggin but he's going to be alright. They got him in room two-twelve next to James' room."

Jonathan walked toward room two-twelve as Jake Rollins came barging out with the nurse right behind him, yelling for him to get back in bed. He almost ran into Jonathan before coming to a stop, saying, "Get this nurse off me Sheriff, I'm gonna get the SOB that blindsided me."

Holding his palm out toward the nurse, Jonathan shook his head, turning to Jake he told him, "No Deputy, you're going to get back in that bed like the nurse says."

"Dammit Sheriff…" Jake said, trying to overrule Jonathan's order, but Jonathan interrupted Rollins with, "Now Deputy, then we talk."

Rollins opened his mouth to argue further but, from the look on the Sheriff's face, he thought better of it and returned to his bed.

Jonathan waited until the deputy was settled back in and the nurse was placated, smiling her thanks to the Sheriff as she quietly left the room.

Sitting down in the straight back chair next to the bed, Jonathan gave Rollins a chance to tell his story.

"Ok Jake, tell me what happened."

"Wayne hadn't no more than disappeared around the corner going to the men's room when James yelled from his room, he needed help. I go charging in and the next thing I know I'm banged from behind. I wake up with Wayne yelling in my ear and shaking me."

"Who did you see in the hall right as you ran in to see what James wanted?" Jonathan asked.

Rollins brow drew together in concentration, finally taking a deep breath he answered, "There was a doctor walking toward me."

"You get a good look at his face?" Jonathan asked.

"No sir, he was looking down at a clip board he had in his hands."

A light switch seemed to click on behind Rollins' eyes as he realized where the Sheriff was leading, "Oh hell, he wasn't no doctor!"

Nodding, Jonathan looked at Hendricks who was standing next to the window asking, "And did you see anyone in the hall when you left for the men's room?"

Shaking his head, Hendricks said, "No sir, no one in the hall and no one passed me. I must have been going in a different direction."

Looking back at Rollins, Jonathan asked him, "What do you remember about the doctor?"

Taking a few moments to gather his thoughts, Rollins told him, "The guy had a doctor-type white coat on. He wasn't tall, about five-eight and his hair was a dusty brown. Hell Sheriff, that's about all I can think of."

Standing, Jonathan gave Rollins a nod telling him, "You stay here overnight and tomorrow you're on desk duty until the doctor gives you the okay."

Not giving Rollins any time to object, he walked to the door telling him over his shoulder, "Call your wife, tell her what happened before she hears from some good citizens. Wayne you're with me."

In the hall, Jonathan turned to the young deputy, "I want you to stay in Winslow's room tonight. Anyone tries to see him, you call me, no one gets in. The deputy on the door is to report to the office, understand?"

Nodding and giving a sharp "Yes sir", Deputy Hendricks turned and headed down the hallway.

Removing his cell phone, Jonathan punches the dispatch number and when the operator answered he instructed, "This is Lawrence. Stop all traffic leaving town, notify the Forest Ranger and the Reservation. Get an APB out on our school janitor and get Chester and Lucas on the interstate with the State Troopers. I'll be back in my office in twenty minutes."

On the way to his office, Jonathan stopped at the city works office, something was bugging him about the 214 bridge. It took only a few minutes to find the last recorded inspection of the 214 County Road Bridge. Finding what had been nagging at him, he ripped the page from the binder and with long strides made his way to Superintendent William Robertson's office. Barging past the receptionist, he pushed the Superintendent's office door open and in two long strides was across the floor, slapping the report down in front of the startled Robertson demanding, "Why the hell did you not tell me that bridge was deemed unsafe three months ago? And why was the bridge not closed and repairs made?"

Jumping to his feet, Robertson tears his eyes from the paper to Jonathan, snapping, "What are you talking about?"

"Three months ago, an inspection was done on the 214 Bridge by Tex-Dot, the report shows a weakness in the structure by the last storm waters that came through there. They recommended it be closed and repairs done before allowing traffic on it again."

Picking up the report that Jonathan slammed down in front of him, Robertson's brows pulled together in a deepening frown. When he finished reading it, he looked up at Jonathan, shaking his head, telling him, "I've never seen this report, where the hell did you get it?"

"I just ripped it out of your files, what do mean you've never seen it before?"

"I mean this damn report has never crossed my desk," Robertson said between gritted teeth as he sat back down with a thud.

Jonathan, for just an instant, wanted to call Robertson a liar but the look on the man's face was enough for any lie detector test. Robertson had not seen the report before this very moment.

"Who would have filed the report?" Jonathan asked as he sat down across from Robertson.

"Julie Mathews, she's the clerk. She's worked for me for nearly ten years, she's good at what she does. Besides she would have had no way of knowing I had not seen it."

"Ok then next question is, who with Tex-Dot hates you enough to bury the report, letting the next flood take care of you?"

Despite the seriousness of the situation Robertson smiled, answering, "Hell, half of the damn state, truth be known."

"Well, the bridge is closed now so you skirted this one. Send your guys out to make sure it is locked down tight. Might want to set someone up tonight to watch and be sure the road closure sawhorses aren't removed."

Straightening, Robertson nods, "Yeah, that I will do." From the anger building deep within him, he added through gritted teeth, "I want this investigated. Sheriff, I want the SOB that did this behind bars."

Standing, Jonathan nodded saying, "Me too, I'll get back to you as soon as I have something. In the meantime, put together the names of anyone who could have done this. It would not have been just your career; people could have been hurt or killed if they were on the bridge when it collapsed."

At the door, Jonathan turned back asking, "Who do you trust at Tex-Dot?"

"Easy one, Virgil Wilson, known him since the third grade. He's a good guy." Was Robertson's prompt answer. Nodding, Jonathan walked out. At the desk he stopped to speak to the attractive middle-aged woman sitting behind the desk. Reading the name plate on her desk, he smiled saying, "Mrs. Downing, I was rude when I came in and for that I hope you can forgive me. Let me know the next ticket you get and I will see about making it go away."

He didn't wait for a reply but the open-mouthed, stunned look on the lady's face was more than enough.

The drive to the courthouse took five minutes. During that short period of time, Jonathan came to a decision. In a split second he hit his breaks, made a sharp U-turn, and headed back to the hospital. Entering the county hospital, he took the elevator up and walked straight to the ICU desk. An attractive RN stepped forward offering to help.

"May I help you Sheriff?"

The tag on the nurse's uniform gave Jonathan her name, giving her a smile, he asked, "Nurse White, I'd like to see the doctor's sign-ins for this morning."

The fact that the sheriff used her name with such pleasant overtones did not impress Nurse White at all. She took several long moments before she handed Jonathan the clipboard with the daily sign-ins by the resident or visiting doctors.

Taking the clipboard, Jonathan scanned the sheets looking for the approximate time of James' disappearance until he found a name, Doctor Benjamin Spencer. Looking back at the nurse, who had been studying him while he reviewed the sign-in sheet, he asked, "Were you present when Dr. Spencer signed in?"

"Yes sir." her answer was given with a small frown.

"Do you personally know Dr. Spencer?" was Jonathan's next question.

The nurse's frown deepened as she answered, "No, I have never seen him before, and Sheriff, I didn't think about it until later but I am not aware of any new doctors with admittance rights being added to our records."

## **CHAPTER 7**

Back at his office Jonathan was growing impatient waiting for the report on Dr. Spencer. He was not surprised to have it come back blank. Doctor Benjamin Spencer did not exist. With that bit of news stuck in his brain he answered his phone, which had rung several times, "Lawrence."

"Sheriff, before you say anything we need to meet." A male voice announced.

It was not hard to recognize Peter James' voice. "Where do you want to meet Mr. James, and before you answer you better have a damn good story to tell."

"You won't be disappointed," James assured Jonathan, adding, "Sheriff, my boy did what he felt he had to."

"Yeah," Jonathan's reply was cold and sarcastic, "It better be really good."

"Meet me and my son at the school's garage in half an hour and I will explain to you."

SCHOOL'S OUT

Jonathan assured him with just a touch of a threat in his voice, "Oh, I'll be there Mr. James, count on it."

Hanging up, Jonathan punched the interoffice phone. When Janie answered, he told her, "I just got a call on my outside line, find out where it was from. And Janie, check the schools to be sure classes have been dismissed."

He did not wait for her response. He disconnected and then punched in Lucas' number, who answered with, "I was just about to call you." Adding quickly, "Couple of cars cruised by, checked them out, nothing so far, I…"

Jonathan interrupted him, "Forget that, I want you in my office, now."

"On my way. What's up," Lucas asked.

"James just called. He wants to meet me at the school's garage. We've got a traitor right here amongst us that we need to find, and James is the key." The heat in Jonathan's words told Lucas all he needed to know. He assured Jonathan, "Be there in ten."

Robertson was going back over and over his conversation with the sheriff. Something about it kept bothering him and he had to figure it out to get any peace of mind. Leaning back in his chair he closed his eyes. He had learned years ago to figure out monumental problems you had to have a free cognizance. It wasn't but a few relaxed minutes until he straightened, and the refrigerator light of knowledge dinged. Reaching for his phone he dialed and waited for a familiar voice to greet him.

"What's on your mind Bill?"

Trying not to sound too giddy, Robertson answered, "You and I need to talk."

There was silence from the other end of the line before a one-word response was made. "Where?"

"I'm going out to the dam, need to check for leaks. Meet you in the control room, say in about half an hour?" Robertson said.

He didn't wait for a response, he didn't need one, Robertson knew he had a meeting.

Jonathan was listening to Christopher James defend his actions and he was beginning to dislike the young man more every minute. The younger James wasn't at all what he had expected. Physically he stood about five-and-half feet tall and probably weighed about one hundred and twenty pounds soaking wet. He had mousey brown hair and faded blue eyes with a Napoleon complex the size of

Mount Everest. It seemed the guy considered himself an excellent shot and only hit what he had aimed for, such as only winging his father slightly in the shoulder, and not hitting any of the deputies that were there. He had to have his father somewhere accessible.

Best of all was the reasoning the SOB gave as his thinking behind all his actions. Christopher James believed he could protect his father better than the Sheriff and all his deputies. This was the last straw for Jonathan who stood as he announced, "Mr. James you are under arrest for attempted murder. Anything you say from this moment forward can and will be used against you…"

Stunned, Christopher James leaped to his feet yelling, "Are you crazy man, I didn't try to kill anyone!"

Jonathan continued, "…in a court of law. If you cannot afford an attorney…" As Jonathan was quoting the Miranda rights, he spun Christopher James around. Grabbing his wrist, he took the handcuffs Lucas was holding out and snapped them on his prisoner, finishing, "one will be appointed by the court. Do you understand these rights as I have quoted them to you?"

"Yeah, yeah I get it, but I didn't try to kill anyone."

Young James' declarations went ignored by Jonathan as he turned to the senior James. Taking another pair of handcuffs from his belt loop and turning James around and pulling his arms back to fasten the second set of cuffs. Without missing a beat, he told James, "And you, Mr. James, are under arrest for murder. You have the same right to remain silent."

Stunned, James shook his head saying, "I didn't kill anyone, Sheriff, you have to believe me."

Taking Peter by the upper right arm, Jonathan nods at Lucas who has the Christopher in a similar grip.

"I am tired of playing games Mr. James, right now you are my best suspect and locking you and your son up is my priority. You can tell me your life story when you're all tucked into a jail cell."

Booking the James men did not take long. Back in his office, Jonathan tried flashing a half smile at Lucas but wasn't sure he managed anything even resembling a smile.

"You don't think James is our killer, do you?" Lucas asked.

Shaking his head, Jonathan knew in his gut that James wasn't and he admitted, "No, I don't but I am going to release a media statement saying he is. We've got twenty-four hours to come up with proof or find the right guy."

"So, where do we start?" Was Lucas' next question.

Looking down at the cell phones that had been removed from the James's at booking, Jonathan nodded, "Well I say we start with the call history of each phone, see where it leads."

Picking up one of the phones, Lucas clicks on the telephone insignia reading the numbers called and especially those with names.

"Why is the name Kullpepper familiar?" Lucas asked, frowning.

"He's the big cheese in town, owns about half of the area and wants the rest." Jonathan answered Lucas adding, "Wonder what the school custodian and Kullpepper have to talk about?"

Looking up from the phone, Lucas smiled, "Better yet, what would the son and Kullpepper have to talk about?" Then telling Jonathan, "This is Junior's cell phone."

Taking the phone, Jonathan pushes the reconnect button saying, "Let's see if we can find out."

Jonathan was disappointed when the call went to Kullpepper's voicemail recording, telling him to leave a message.

"Mr. Kullpepper, this is Sheriff Lawrence. I need to speak with you concerning a matter of importance, please give me a call."

"Well if the big cheese was talking about something with young James that he wanted to keep quiet, he could get his shorts in a wad hearing from you on the kid's phone." Lucas said with a smile.

Taking a deep breath, Jonathan let it out slowly, then changed the subject, "Right now, I am going to check to be sure that the people along the river have been evacuated."

Standing, Lucas offered, "Why don't I take a run by and check it out? I'm headed back to the ranch to check on a couple of mares due to foal any minute."

Nodding his head, Jonathan gladly agreed, "Sounds like a good idea to me. How many foals have been birthed since the first shipment of pregnant mares?"

"Adding these two, it will make six. Some pretty good-looking ones, so far."

After walking Lucas out of the courthouse, Jonathan turned and went back to his office. It was still bugging him as to what the young James would have to talk to Kullpepper about. Going to the cellblock, he stood in front of Christopher James' cell door. The young James was laying stretched out on the small cot when the Sheriff walked up. He rose to his feet and walked over to stand in front of Jonathan asking, "Am I being released?"

Jonathan shook his head, "That's up to the judge. What did you have to talk to Kullpepper about? And don't try and tell me you didn't talk to him, it's on your cell phone."

Hesitating for a moment, the younger man took a deep breath and told him, "Believe it or not Sheriff, I am a licensed Pediatric specialist, I am in private practice, my patients are adolescents. Mr. Kullpepper's fifteen-year old daughter is a patient. We were talking about his daughter."

Studying James' expression and slight change of tone, Jonathan knows he was not going to like the answer as he asked, "Why were you treating the daughter?"

This time James balked, saying, "Doctor-patient privilege, Sheriff. You will have to ask Mr. Kullpepper that."

As much as Jonathan hated to admit it, he respected James more for refusing to violate the physician's code of ethics. So, with a tone of voice just a little bit friendlier he asked, "So, what can you tell me about the reason for the treatment? And does it have anything to do with what is going on in my town right now?"

James took a deep breath, considering the question carefully before answering, "To do with your murder case? I don't know. But as far as being my patient, she seems to have a poor sense of balance and has had some pretty serious injuries for a fifteen-year old girl."

A cold sliver of ice ran down Jonathan's spine as he thanked James and told him, "I'll see if I can get the judge to listen to your story as to why you did what you did and maybe go light on you."

Smiling, James said, "Thanks Sheriff. I have to admit, I did a pretty stupid thing and I could have hurt one of your deputies."

Jonathan nodded and walked away, his mind already turning in circles with questions. If Kullpepper was a child abuser, how far removed would the theory be that he could also be a killer?

SCHOOL'S OUT

Back at his office, he stopped to ask Janie, "Do you know the Kullpepper girl?"

At her nod and soft "Yes sir" he asked, "Are you two friends?" Janie shook her head no, telling him, "I'm two years ahead of Cathy. Why do you ask Sheriff?"

Janie's soft question and the tentative why she asks her question set the alarms going off in Jonathans' head.

"What can you tell me about Cathy Kullpepper?" was his next question.

"Cathy is quiet, she doesn't seem to have too many friends. Not any I've seen her hanging out with, anyway. I don't think she has ever been in any kind of trouble, not that I know of." Janie paused and added, "My mom is a psychologist, Sheriff, and she talks to me a lot about things I should watch for in others. To be able to help someone who might not know how to ask."

If he was surprised about what Janie said, Jonathan showed no sign of it as he asked, "And what have you noticed about Cathy Kullpepper that bothers you?"

Taking a deep breath, Janie blurted, "I think one of Cathy's parents is abusing her."

Smiling at her, Jonathan told her, "Thank you Janie and this stays just between you and me."

As Jonathan turned to go back into his office, Janie asked, "Are you going to help Cathy, Sheriff?"

Nodding, he answered, "Yes, I am."

As he entered his office, he did not see the big 'thank you' smile on Janie's face.

Sitting down at his desk, Jonathan glanced at the clock. Fifteen minutes before the well would be shut down. He wanted to talk to Nancy Williamson, the school's principal, for the past ten years. Nancy was in her late fifties, she was short, standing only about five feet four inches with salt and pepper hair but the prettiest flashing black eyes he had ever seen. There wasn't anyone who disliked Nancy and that included the kids she had to discipline. He and Nancy had met several times in the past few years to discuss one of her kids that she felt was straying from the right pathway. She depended on Jonathan to talk with and readjust her straying student.

When she answered, Nancy's voice showed some of the strain she was feeling because of her concern for her "kids" with the threat of flooding. Not wanting to take up too much of her time, Jonathan opened with, "It's Jonathan Lawrence. I'm sorry to be calling right now, Nancy but I have a question."

"Jonathan, as many times as I have bothered you at inconvenient times, trust me it's ok." Nancy assured him.

Wasting no time, Jonathan asked, "What can you tell me about your student Cathy Kullpepper?"

Nancy paused a moment before answering, "Cathy is a quiet, well-behaved ninth grader. She maintains a B average but with a little more effort could be a straight-A honor roll student. And as far as I am aware, she has very few, if any, close friends. Why do you ask Jonathan?"

Ignoring Nancy's question, he asked, "Do you know anything about her home life?"

This time there was a longer pause before she told Jonathan in a lower, softer tone, "I do not think Cathy's home life is a happy one. She gives all the signs of being an abused child but I have no proof. Not enough to alert the law anyway."

Taking a deep breath, Jonathan released it slowly saying, "Thanks Nancy, this will help me. I promise your name won't be mentioned. But, can you tell me what makes you think Cathy has been abused?"

Nancy made no hesitation in answering Jonathan's question, "She has too many absences. She seems to have chronic stomach problems and she wears too many long-sleeved blouses for a fifteen-year-old girl." Before Jonathan can form any kind of a reply, she added, "And, Jonathan, her beautiful eyes are always so sad looking."

"Again, thank you, Nancy. I promise you I will handle this." she realized that the promise of handling it was made sincerely and his words were not to be taken lightly. Her voice was almost a whisper as she said, "God bless you Jonathan."

Walking the top of the spillway, Robertson mentally checked the open gates and silently calculated the amount of water flowing through them. As long as the rain continued to hold, he figured the floodwaters would descend back down to normal in twenty-four hours. Of course, then the gates would have to be cleaned. Robertson took a deep breath, releasing it slowly, saying, "I've just about had enough of this sh-..." Hearing footsteps behind him, he turned, a look of stunned surprise on his face. He opened his mouth to say, "What the hell…" And was cut short as the echoing sound of a shot echoed though the East Texas woods, a bullet slamming into Robertson's chest. The impact was powerful enough that Robertson was knocked backward, sending him off the dam and over into the spillway.

The shadows were deep enough that if there had been an observer, it would have been nearly impossible to describe the figure. Other than it did not give the appearance of a big person.

## **CHAPTER 8**

Standing on the courthouse steps, Jonathan was glad the press conference was over. Now all he had to do was watch the half hour worth of videotape that Chester and Sanchez had recorded. He really wasn't expecting anything to jump out at him but he could hope for maybe some kind of quirk to show up that might give a place to start looking. Right now, they were at a dead end.

Going back into his office, Jonathan sat at his desk, staring at the files spread out before him. Studying each of the shots of the schoolhouse, reading the statement of the James over again for the fourth time, Jonathan knew there was something he was missing, there had to be.

Leaning back in his chair he closed his eyes. He was developing one hell of a headache, in more ways than one. It was not a sudden bolt of lightning but Jonathan figured he would take what he could get. Unclipping his cell from his belt, he pushes Phil Sheridan's number. When Sheridan answered, Jonathan wasted no time in letting him know what he needed.

"How soon can you get me airport video footage of the flights going in and out of each of the cities where one of the sleepers were killed?"

Sheridan fell silent for a few moments before asking, "How many days before and after do you want?"

"Well, seeing as to how our guy wouldn't want to stick around town after the body was discovered, I'd say no more than two days after. And, before, if he has any brains at all, which he does, five days at the most."

"You think about the fact your guy could have driven or even taken a bus?" Sheridan questioned.

"Yeah, I thought about it but, if it was me, I want to get in there and get out as quick as I could. The longer I stick around, the more chances there are that someone will notice and remember me when the police come around asking questions."

"You also think about the number of travelers in and out of an airport in a twenty-four-hour period?"

"Yeah, I thought about that too. Chester, Lucas and I will be anchored for several days and that's where I come to my second favor. I need you to take charge of my two prisoners, the older man is a Russian spy and his son is an accomplice so they should be in federal hands anyway."

"Hell Jonathan," Sheridan knew he was going to lose the argument before he even started, so instead of ranting he takes a deep breath, releasing it in one puff and said, "I'll put a couple of my guys in your jail cell, we'll keep the guy alive for you but I'm warning you, you had better be quick."

Smiling, Jonathan told him, "I owe you big time Phil and we will not sleep until all the tapes are reviewed."

"Yeah, yeah, just make it quick." Sheridan told him and then added, "I'll have the tapes delivered by my guys when they come, be a couple of days."

Disappointed at the time frame, Jonathan let it pass knowing full well that Sheridan would do his best as fast as possible.

Clipping the cell phone back on his belt, Jonathan knew the next few days were going to be nerve-wracking. To sit and do nothing to find out who their perp is would be trying. So, he figured he might as well spend the time constructively and find a way to talk to the Kullpepper girl.

If Cathy Kullpepper was being molested or physically assaulted by her father, he wanted the scumbag now.

Glancing at the clock on his office wall, Jonathan was surprised to find it was already past five. There was nothing more he could do tonight, the James's were locked up and safe from harm, and the latest report from the hospital on Deputy Mark Winslow was not good. He was still unconscious and still on life support.

Walking in the front door of his house, Jonathan took a deep breath of the sweet aroma floating through the house, and he knew deep in his bones Samantha was home and in the kitchen.

Finding her at the sink busy washing up the muffin pan she had just emptied of fresh-from-the-oven blueberry muffins. Jonathan walked over to stand behind Sam, placing his arms around her waist as he leaned in and kissed the nape of her neck.

"How did you know I was thirsting for a blueberry muffin?"

Smiling, Sam leaned back against him, telling him, "Because that's the only thing you usually have on your mind."

Nibbling on her soft earlobe, Jonathan managed to murmur, "Uhun, not the only thing," as his right hand started a slow crawl up to cup her breast.

Slapping his hand away, Sam scowled at him, "Behave yourself! We have company."

Stepping back, Jonathan asked, "Company? Who?"

Before Sam could answer, a masculine voice spoke from behind him, "I guess that would be me Jonathan."

Turning to face the recognizable voice of Governor Mark Browning, a sudden apprehensive shiver ran up and down Jonathan's spine. Stretching his hand forward, Jonathan wasted little time in asking, "Governor, it's good seeing you but what the hell brings you?"

Laughing, Browning pointed at Samantha, "Your wife informed me that if I wanted you to listen to a cockamamie idea I have, then I'd better come and propose it in person."

Glancing at Sam, it was hard to read her expression right at that moment but of one thing he was sure, from the firm set of her jaw he knew whatever the Governor wanted, she was totally against it.

Looking back at the Governor, Jonathan nodded and started toward the kitchen exit, saying, "I think you and I need to talk in my office." Looking back at his wife, Jonathan said, "Tell Lucas I want him here, please."

Not waiting for her reply, he led the way to his office. He wanted Lucas involved in listening to Browning. Having worked for the Governor, Jonathan figured Lucas would be able to read the depth of whatever Browning had worked out.

Seated behind his desk, Jonathan nodded at the Governor, telling him, "Alright Mark, you've got the floor."

The Governor knew right at this moment Jonathan was not in a happy mood and he understood why. Samantha had been taken as a confidante against him and kept secret talks that she, if he were Jonathan, would be pissed off too, so, he had to make his pitch good.

"I am not running for Governor, instead I am running for state Senator and I need your help. As Governor, I have fought those that are trying to destroy our lifestyle, our homes, our state and our government. I have seen people's lives and businesses destroyed by corrupt government officials, by foreign heads of state, by the drug cartel. I saw you, your family, and your friends, come in, totally unknown to the outsiders, and take the corrupt down. You answered to no government, to no man other than yourself and your honor. I want that type of a group that I, and any law-abiding citizen, can call on for help when they see themselves sinking in a tar pit not of their making. No matter what country, no matter who they are, if they are on the side of right you and your people will fight for them."

Taking a deep breath, the Governor managed a small smile as he added, "And, I don't want to make you angry or upset with Sam, she tried to make things easier for me, and you, by keeping this visit a secret. Only you, Lucas, Joseph and his bride."

As the Governor mentioned Joseph's name, the office door opened, and Joseph Skywolf entered. His long black hair hung in thick braids, and he was dressed in denim and black boots. Joseph walked toward Jonathan, his hand stuck out, a big smile on his face as he said, "Happy to see you too, Boss. And no, I didn't know why we came home early. Not until today, Lilly kept it to herself. We might need to have a talk with our women folk."

Standing, Jonathan walked around his desk to shake the hand Joseph was holding out, saying "Yeah, that seems like it is in order."

Turning so that all three men were in his complete circle of vision, Jonathan was not sure what to think about everything that the Governor had said so far. He knew he had a lot of questions running through his brain, but they did not seem to be in much order.

"Governor, I have a handful of questions and I am sure Lucas and Joseph have as well. What they are right this moment, I cannot honestly say but I would say you have a lot more to tell us. So why don't you begin with what you visualize this superhero group to be, exactly."

The Governor took a few moments to study each of the three men before telling them his vision. Half an hour later, Jonathan stood up and walked toward the office door telling them, "Gentlemen I think we could all stand a short break. I am sure the ladies have drinks and snacks of some kind waiting." Holding the door open, he looked the Governor in the eye, telling him, "Mark I would like to meet with Joseph and Lucas a bit before you rejoin us."

The Governor nodded; he understood the request. He had hope that it would not put more barriers in the pathway. Leaving the office, he went off in search of Lillian and Samantha.

Closing the door behind the Governor, Jonathan turned back to face his two deputies and friends with one question, "Well?"

Joseph was first to speak, "White Chief leave much out." said with a grin.

Lucas nodded, "Yeah, I'd say our friend left a lot of details out but I worked for the Gov. He's fair dinkum as far as I'm concerned."

Nodding, Jonathan agreed with Lucas. He knew Mark Browning was an honest man. A man to be trusted but, there was always a "but."

"I have an idea the Governor has everything figured out right down to every I dotted, and every T crossed." Lucas said, adding, "you know with the new program we got started with these Mustangs, it would be a perfect cover, traveling around the country even the entire globe. Talking about the Mustang building a breeding base."

Frowning, Joseph grunted, "Humph, sounds like you are all in for this White eye madness, my Australian Bushman."

"And you're not?" Lucas fired back.

"Once in a while, I've thought about what it would be like to roam the country, hey, as a dumb redskin I could be a real good spy." Joseph answered with a twisted smile.

"Well," Jonathan said, putting a stop to their banter, "I want to hear all the things Mark hasn't told us. So, what say you we take that break and meet back in about ten minutes."

The three were past being ready for a break which was evident when they had no argument to offer against it.

## **CHAPTER 9**

While the others gladly sat at the dining table enjoying an evening feast that Samantha and Lillian prepared, Jonathan chose to walk outside. Standing on the front porch, he leaned against a pillar, sipping a fresh cup of hot coffee. His back was to the door when he heard it open, there was no need to turn around, he knew it was Samantha. She walked up, placing her arms around his waist, and leaned against him softly saying, "I'm sorry for not telling you…"

Before she could say anything else, Jonathan interrupted, "It's alright I understand." Lifting her hands, he kissed the top of each before warning, "But don't ever keep something like this from me again."

Standing back, Samantha walked around in front of him, saying, "I promise." Turning to leave, she stopped and looked back over her shoulder with a smile to ask, "Does that apply to if I were pregnant as well?"

Samantha's confession was just at the moment that Jonathan took a swallow of his coffee, which was spewed out in a shower just missing Samantha. He just managed to stammer, "P-pregnant!"

Moving back into the circle of his arms, Samantha said softly, "Yes Jonathan, pregnant."

Still stunned, Jonathan gasped, "When, how…"

Laughing, Samantha scolded playfully, "Well really Jonathan, I thought you would surely know how it happens? You are over sixteen. We're expecting a child. As to when, in seven months."

Jonathan remained quiet, his eyes never leaving hers. It was evident that he was thrilled with her news, but a frown was beginning to pull his brows down. Holding her at arm's length, he asked, "Is everything alright, no problems or anything?"

Shaking her head, Samantha assured him everything was fine. "You're okay with this aren't you?" she asked.

"Okay? I'm stunned, ecstatic, lost for words, and I want to yell it from the tallest mountain. That covers it a little."

With a smile stretching her lips even wider, Samantha tried not to cry from his reaction.

"I wasn't going to tell you until everyone was gone but you were so hurt that I had kept the meeting with Mark a secret, I had to make you smile again."

Hugging her to him, Jonathan took a deep breath, releasing it slowly before he answered.

"It's okay, it isn't you I have a problem with, it's Mark for infringing on friendship. He and I will talk."

Stepping back from the circle of his arms, Samantha brushed away the tears from her cheek, smiling she reminded Jonathan, "Just remember that Mark has gone through some rough times with some that he trusted. He kind of figures you are the one person he can trust, and he wanted to be here to tell you himself what he would like to see happen. So, don't be too tough on him."

"And you think this is something I should really consider getting involved with?"

"My personal opinion is no, but I know you well enough to know you will make your own decision and I will accept that."

"Why do you think I should not do this?" Jonathan asked, wondering himself if this idea of the Governor's was something he should pass on.

Smiling, Samantha answered his question with as much honesty she could muster. "Because I like having you around and I know being the Sheriff of a small rural town is not as exciting as this other thing might sound, but it is no walk in the park here. Not where your safety is concerned. But whatever decision you make is okay, I promise."

Taking her hand, Jonathan kissed her forehead saying, "Okay let's go get this over with."

Walking back into the dinning-room, their appearance brought silence to the room. The Governor, Lucas, Joseph and Lillian all seemed to be holding their breath, waiting for Jonathan to speak.

"I think the Governor has some more information he needs to talk about so why don't we...," Jonathan began, stopping and turning to face Samantha before continuing, "...which includes Sam and Lillian, retire to the den and let's hear him out."

With all sitting quietly, their eyes glued on him, the Governor goes on to explain his idea of an international security firm which would provide private investigatory services of federal and state litigation, executive protection nationally and internationally, and proactively addressing areas of risk and vulnerability. The personnel of this company would be highly capable, reliable, honorable people with years of experience. Each would have an intensive background investigation before being brought in as an agent. The work would be sealed and confidential, for their leader's eyes only. The leader and head of the organization would be Jonathan.

Stopping, the Governor took a deep breath, letting it out slowly as he studied each of the faces before him. None of them gave any indication of their thoughts or their feelings toward what now seemed like a wild idea. He took a deep breath of relief when Jonathan spoke up asking, "What gave you this crazy idea Mark?"

"Well you did, actually," the governor told him, adding, "You most likely don't remember, we were at the hospital, in the hall, waiting on the latest on Lucas. I mentioned to you how fed up I was with having to question the facts of investigations being done on moles in our government. You laughed and said there needed to be a bunch of goons that weren't for sale and who cared nothing about whose toes they stepped on getting to the core of justice."

Looking at each of those assembled, the Governor's smile broadened, "I reckon that pretty much covers you guys."

Before anyone could raise any kind of question, Jonathan's cell phone went off. Removing it from his belt, Jonathan rose and walked out of the room as he answered, "Lawrence."

"Sheriff, this is Nurse White at the county hospital. I'm sorry to have to tell you, your deputy passed ten minutes ago."

Letting the nurses' words sink in, Jonathan took a deep breath, releasing it slowly before saying, "Thank you, I appreciate you letting me know. Have you notified the coroner's office?"

"Yes sir, I called them first." She assured him.

Opening his mouth to thank her once again, Jonathan stopped and instead asked, "Did anyone come in asking about Deputy Winslow or try to see him?"

There was moment of silence as the nurse thought back over the day, finally she answered telling him, "The County Attorney Mr. Golightly inquired as to how Deputy Winslow was doing when he visited the hospital earlier. And as far as visitors, your young deputy was at the door and he allowed no one other than a nurse or doctor." With a soft laugh she added, "And he checked their ID before allowing them to enter."

Satisfied, Jonathan thanked her and went back into the den to join the others. It was not hard for the assembled group to know something had happened from the look of sadness on Jonathan's face. It wasn't going to be good news. Not waiting for anyone to ask Jonathan announced, "Deputy Mark Winslow passed away about half-an-hour ago. I am sorry Governor, but I need to see the Winslow family."

Standing, the Governor gave Jonathan a nod, saying, "Of course Jonathan, don't worry." Glancing at Samantha, he added, "If Samantha will have me, I'll be here waiting when you get back."

Lucas stood with Joseph, telling Jonathan, "We're going with you. We'll all come back here and finish up the talks."

Thankful for their support, Jonathan smiled at the two, saying, "Thank you I appreciate the thought but Lucas you have a mare about to foal, maybe you should stay."

Shaking his head, Lucas informed him. "Janie and one of the young guys working here, Pete, can take care and do whatever I would be called on to do. Mark was a good bloke to have on your backside, I need to be there."

Nodding, Jonathan smiled at Samantha, walking over to her and kissed her cheek, softly whispering, "Love you, keep the light on." Before the tears pooling in her eyes could spill over, he turned and walked out.

Joseph, who had been standing next to Lillian, looked at her and with a slight grin said, "*mehohta htse'eme*." Following Jonathan and Lucas.

The drive to town from the ranch normally took thirty minutes, depending on the weather, which was more than enough time for Jonathan to ask a question of his two deputies and friends.

"I know there hasn't been a lot of time to think but I want to hear your thoughts."

Lucas was the first one to speak up, "I can see where it might be a great chance to do some good on a bigger scale than in a small rural town or even a city the size of Houston. But, I'm small town country. I don't feel like being gone from the ranch for long periods of time… but an assignment every once in a while, doesn't sound so bad." With a sheepish grin he finished with, "Know I'm not indispensable but I figure the mustangs depend on me and I kind of like that."

Joseph nodded understandingly as he gave his point of view. "I belong in these woods and in this town, that's how I feel. I don't care for big cities or big people but, *Ese'e* Jonathan, it is your call. *Ese'e* Lucas and I could keep the light burning in your window when you're away and you can do the same for us."

Jonathan laughed, thanking Joseph, "Appreciate that thought but some recent news has me unsure. I kind of like this small-town life even with crazies running around but by the next election you could see me unemployed. I don't really like the thought of money being freely given from sources we are not aware of. I trust the Governor, he says there are no strings, but just how sure is that?"

"What do you think the Governor will do if we don't take him up on this idea of his?" Lucas asked.

"Well," Jonathan took a deep breath saying, "my first thought is, he will not give up. He is really behind this idea. If you two agree, I will point out that the major problem I have with it is the unknown source of the funding."

Both Joseph and Lucas nodded and said, "We agree on that," as though synchronized.

"Ok, I'll say we agree on that issue. Some recent news has me thinking about making a change. These twenty-four hours a day, seven days a week doesn't give a person much time for anything else. And, like I said, the next election could see a new Sheriff in town. And, from some news I was given today I don't really relish the idea of unemployment."

Figuring it was time for some good news, a big smile spread over Joseph's face. Asking, "You going to tell

Lucas and me what this news is that has you wanting to secure your future a little better?"

"Hell, Joseph I figure you already know, seeing as our squaws have been together for the better part of the day." Jonathan responded.

Joseph slapped Jonathan on the shoulder laughing, "Well you know she had to tell me. Congratulations, old man."

"Well since I haven't spent the better part of the day with your two squaws maybe you could fill me in?" Lucas suggested.

Before Jonathan could answer Joseph said, "*Htse'eme* Jonathan is gonna be a papa."

Lucas' surprise was certainly obvious and he was equally as excited. "Alright ole' cobber, you gonna be a daddy!"

"Thanks fellows, it's good to know that you two will be around to play God-Parent."

The drive to the hospital seemed quick for the three men as they were enjoying making future plans for Jonathan and Samantha's papoose.

(*Htse'e:* friend, *Mehohta:* love, *Htse'eme*: friend. - Native American) (ole' cobber - Australian)


Entering the waiting room on the ICU floor, it was easy to locate Patricia Winslow. She was standing in the warm, comforting circle of her family and friends. Seeing the sheriff and the two deputies, she walked toward them, a sad smile on her lips. The widow was an attractive, forty-year-old brunette, her brown eyes swimming in a pool of tears. The normally immaculately dressed woman was dressed in jeans, an oversized sweatshirt and tennis shoes. She wore no makeup, which showed both her stress and age. Holding her hand out toward Jonathan, she expressed her appreciation, "Thank you, Sheriff, for coming," she looked at Lucas and Joseph as she spoke, it was evident her words were meant for all three men. They each, in turn, expressed their condolences for their friend, co-worker and her husband's passing.

Taking her hand, Jonathan leaned forward and kissed her cheek, "If there is anything, we can do…"

Patricia Winslow cut him short, "I know I can rely on you and your deputies. Tell me Sheriff, do you have any idea who did this and why?"

Jonathan answered with regret, "Not yet, but I promise you we will find who killed Mark."

Nodding, she looked back over her shoulder at the group waiting for her return. Turning back to Jonathan, she said, "I know you will. I have to get back to Mark's parents, they are taking this hard."

Smiling at the three men, she turned and walked back to the family circle. Watching her walk away, Jonathan removed his cell phone and called the dispatcher. When they answered, he instructed, "This is Lawrence, I want a squad car with two deputies at the county hospital. They are to be escorts for Patricia Winslow and her family. They are to stay with the Winslow's until relieved."

An hour later Jonathan, Joseph and Lucas were back in the den at the ranch. It did not take Jonathan long to tell the Governor their thoughts pertaining to the source of the funding. From the disappointed look on the Governor's face, it was obvious he was unhappy but before he could make any sort of reply or plea, Jonathan endeavored to help the Governor accept their concern.

"Mark, you know we consider you a friend, and we would be there for you anytime but," glancing from Joseph to Lucas who each nodded, agreeing with him, Jonathan continued, "to be honest we do not take to the idea of money being given willy-nilly from someone we have no knowledge of. It does not sound inviting."

Joseph and Lucas join in a chorus of "Yeah", endorsing Jonathan. The Governor privately applauded the three men and their questioning of the investors.

The men putting up the money were men he trusted and he would not have approached Jonathan with the idea if he had doubts. He tried to express his feelings, "I do understand and if I did not know these men, know them as well as I do myself, I would not suggest this to you. Jonathan, if I privately introduced you to each man and you were to ask them any and all questions that you have, would you do so? Keeping in mind that they will not want it known they are the backers, ever."

Looking from Joseph to Lucas, he waited for their nod of agreement before he gave the governor the answer he sought.

"Yes. Understanding that there are no questions off the table? Also, I would prefer the funds not be a gift but a loan to start up such a firm with a plan to pay it back in five years, which would include a three percent interest."

Looking from Lucas to Joseph, he told them, "The loan would be in my name, you two are not obligated in any way. It's the only way to do this kind of thing."

Glancing one to the other, Joseph spoke first, "Naw, in for an ounce in for a pound, my name's on that loan, too."

Nodding, Lucas joined in, "Me too mate, I'm in all the way."

Jonathan felt choked up, but his hand was firm as he shook the hand of each prospective partner.

Surprise was not half of what the Governor felt. Standing, he held his hand out to each man, giving a firm handshake of his commitment.

Lucas was the first to speak, "Governor, I like and respect you and I hope things are as you believe. Now if you blokes will excuse me, I've got me a foal to check on."

Waiting until after Lucas left, Joseph added his input, "Governor, don't know you really well but what I know, I like. Just promise me you don't speak with a forked tongue."

Laughing, the Governor shook Joseph's hand telling him, "I do not speak with a forked tongue, ever, I promise."

Samantha and Lilly entered the room as each of the men were saying their goodbyes and thanks. Leading the way out the front entrance, Jonathan stood aside placing his arm around Samantha's waist, as they watched their friends drive off.

Looking down at Samantha, who was nestled next to him, he smiled saying, "It's been a long day, what say we retire for the night and you sing me to sleep with the lullaby you will sing to our son?"

"Oh, so you know we are having a boy?" She asked with a laugh.

Holding the door open for her, Jonathan said, "My mama once told me you can tell the sex of a baby that a woman is carrying by looking at her butt. If it's a boy the butt will be round." Slapping Samantha gently on the butt as she entered the doorway ahead of him, he told her, "And lady yours is most certainly round."

## CHAPTER 10

The telephone ringing was a rude awaking. Jonathan, his half open eyes automatically look at the bedside clock. It said nine o'clock, he had slept well past his normal seven. It took another jarring ring before he reached for the phone and answered in a low growl, "Lawrence." The ringing woke Samantha as well. Rolling over on her opposite side away from Jonathan's growl, she buried her head under her pillow.

Jonathan sat up, throwing his legs off of the bed in one swift movement as he heard Chester's voice saying, "Sheriff, I'm out on County 22 North at the embankment that leads off down to the river, we've got a body tangled up in the tree roots. It's Bill Robertson, he's been shot Sheriff."

Jonathan's "Hell" was louder than he had intended. He had not wanted to wake Samantha, that thought was wasted as she sat up with a jerk.

"Don't touch anything until the coroner gets finished, I'll be there in thirty minutes." Jonathan instructed as Samantha sat up in bed. She watched Jonathan dress, a frown pulling her brows together, she inquired, "What's happened?"

Sitting down beside her, Jonathan leaned over and kissed her on the forehead. Straightening up he told her, "They found Bill Robertson's body off County Road 22, down by the river. He'd been shot."

Taking a deep breath, Samantha knew the answer before she asked but she put her question into words. "Should I meet you back at the courthouse for a statement?"

Nodding, Jonathan stood, telling her, "Give me three hours and I'll release what we have or as much as I can."

Nodding, Samantha closed her eyes as her next question was said sadly, "What's happening to this town Jon? We're a small rural community made up of friends and family. We are not New York or Chicago."

Samantha's words plagued him all the way to the waiting crime scene. The idea of looking at the occurring events at different angles had not been visited. Two different stories, two different perps.

Getting out of his car, Jonathan greeted Chester, "What do we know so far?"

"The coroner says Robertson has not been dead more than a couple of hours." Falling in step beside the sheriff Chester says, "One bullet in the head, he was dead when he hit the water. Considering the depth and flow of the river, I'd say he took the hit up top of the dam. Also, Sheriff, the gates were opened in the same time frame as the shooting."

Jonathan's eyes followed the flow of the river as far as the tree line would allow.

"So, Robertson opens the flood gates, goes up on top of the dam to watch the outflow and whoever shot him is waiting there for him." Turning slowly, Jonathan eyes follow the perimeter of the big dam. "The perp knew there need be no concern of anyone seeing anything. So, our shooter is very familiar with the dam. Traffic crossing the causeway would not pay any attention to someone on the dam. First of all, any passer-by would be too concerned with getting home and making sure everything is secure."

Seeing Chester's frown, Jonathan explained, "The shooter is someone who knew Roberts, knew the dam, knew the entire area, and is familiar with guns. One shot in the head, they knew Robertson would come out on top of the dam once the floodgates were opened. Our perp went to the dam and waited."

"Damn Sheriff, the shooter knew Robertson? Who hated him that much to want him dead?" Chester asked.

"That's a question I don't have an answer for, yet. Have a couple of deputies search the dam, each end of it. I want every little piece of anything that does not fit with the grounds brought in. Look for tracks, animal or human, make a plastic imprint of any human track. If you can't get an imprint, take snaps up close."

"What are you going to do Sheriff?" was Chester's question.

Taking a deep breath, Jonathan said, "Go tell Bill's wife. Call me if you find anything."

Following Wendy Robertson into the living room, Jonathan was surprised to see the elegant furnishings throughout the modest brick home.

When the Widow Robertson motioned for him to have a seat, Jonathan declined. First, because he did not want to be seated when he told the young widow her husband had died. In addition to that was the tingle that was beginning to crawl up the back of his neck. The widow Robertson was at least twenty years younger than her husband. She was a striking brunette with deep blue eyes and a voluptuous figure, not the kind of woman Jonathan thought would have married Robertson. She was still in her robe that appeared to the Sheriff like she had just thrown the robe on. Considering the time of day, Jonathan could not help but to wonder why the widow Robertson had just gotten out of bed. Wishing there was an easier way to break the bad news, he said, "Mrs. Robertson, perhaps you should be seated."

Sitting down in a pale blue velvet French back chair, she looked up at him, her eyes widening. "You're frightening me, Sheriff, what is it?"

"I'm sorry to have to tell you this but your husband was shot and killed yesterday." He told her, never taking his eyes off of her face.

She sat still and quiet for several moments, staring at the sheriff. Finally shaking her head, she forced a smile saying, "I'm sorry, Sheriff. You've made a mistake. Bill has no enemies that would want him dead." Taking a deep breath, she released it slowly as she stood up. "No, you have made a mistake." She repeated.

"No, Mrs. Robertson, there has been no mistake." Jonathan assured her then he asked, "Is there someone I can call to have come and be with you?"

Shaking her head, she reassured him, "No, no. Thank you. I will call my mother, she will come."

Opening the front door, she stepped back, allowing Jonathan to walk out. A small smile touched her lips as she held her hand out to him, she said, "Thank you, Sheriff, for coming."

Her hand is small and soft, Jonathan could not help but to notice how perfectly manicured her nails were. Dropping her hand, he stepped back saying, "If I, or any member of the Sheriff's office, can help you in any way be sure and let us know."

Wendy Robertson stood in the doorway watching until Jonathan had backed out the driveway and pulled away.

She then softly closed the door and the click of the lock seem to echo down the drive.

Back in his office Jonathan sat quietly staring across the room at the painting of the Trinity River Bridge that had been commissioned during the final year of its construction. If someone were to ask him what he saw that was so interesting in the painting, he could not have given an answer. He was not really seeing the painting but recalling his meeting with Bill Robertson's widow. The young widow had not asked any questions. Yes, she could have been in shock as the news set in but, and there is always a 'but', she had ushered him out hurriedly. There were a lot of questions he needed to ask the widow Robertson, but they could wait.

Pushing the intercom button to his reception desk he was somewhat surprised to hear Lillian's "Morning Boss".

"Didn't expect you in today," was his response, asking, "Thought you and Joseph were still on your honeymoon time?"

"Me too," then there was a soft laugh and her reply, "Curtis called Joseph out to see if he could pick up any tracks or see something he and the other deputies might have missed at your latest. So, figured I might as well come in."

"Where did you send Janie off to?"

"Oh, she ran off soon as my head came through the door. Seems she has some horses she wants to play with. What can I do for you?"

Smiling, Jonathan wanted to tell her he was happy to have her back but knowing Lillian, he let it slide and said, "Start a complete background check on Bill Robertson. Include his finances as well as his wife. What deputies do we have on call?"

Lillian was quick with her answer, "Virgil Wilson and his cousin Lee. And Boss you got a young man out here waiting for you, Martin Sanchez."

"Send Sanchez in and then get Virgil and his cousin Lee out to Bill Robertson's subdivision. I want them to canvas the neighborhood, see if anyone overheard, saw or even thought they saw or heard anything in the area around Robertson's house."

Lillian acknowledged his orders with a "will do."

Getting up, Jonathan walked over and opened his office door, allowing Sanchez to enter. Pointing to a chair in front of his desk Jonathan said, "Have a seat and tell me what brings you to my office. Hope it's not to have a traffic ticket fixed."

Grinning, Sanchez assured him it was not, "No Sir, but I was talking with Chester and he says I might be able to get on with the Sheriff Department. I thought I would talk to you and see if there might be a chance."

Studying Sanchez for a few moments, Jonathan finally nodded, telling him, "Well assuming you're over twenty-one, no felony arrests, no warrants outstanding and you have a high school diploma, I'd say you have a pretty good chance."

Shaking his head, Sanchez took a deep breath saying, "I guess I was expecting too much. I never finished high school, Sheriff. Dropped out three months into my senior year."

"You mind telling me why?"

"My mom was really sick, and pop was working two shifts to feed and house us, plus paying for Mom's medical care. So, I quit and got a job to help out."

Hearing Sanchez's story made Jonathan's mind up quickly. Punching Lillian's intercom number, he waited and when she answered, he instructed, "Lillian get a hold of the high school superintendent and set up a GED test for Martin Sanchez two weeks from today."

Not waiting for Lillian's reply, Jonathan stood and walked around his desk, holding his hand out toward Sanchez and told him, "You have two weeks. Get to the library to do some studying, go take the test, and then come back here and we'll get you into the academy."

Standing, Sanchez shook Jonathan's hand gratefully, "You assuming I will past the GED?" Was his stunned query.

Walking over to the door, Jonathan opened it, telling Sanchez, "Yeah, I expect no less."

Following Sanchez, he stood and watched him walk out before going to see Lillian. It wasn't that he didn't like Janie, she did a good job, but Lillian was really the Sheriff's office anchor, his anyway. Ending her call as Jonathan walked up, she smiled at him saying, "Martin will make a good deputy."

"Yeah, I think so. You might offer to tutor him some on subjects he might need refreshing on in order for him to make a higher grade."

Nodding, Lillian did not need to make any kind of a verbal reply. Jonathan knew she had already planned on doing that very thing.

"I'm going out to the dam, let Chester know."

Once again Jonathan knew he did not need to wait for or expect a reply, Lillian was already on the phone following his wishes.

Driving out to the dam gave Jonathan time to think over all the happenings in the last twenty-four hours. It all seemed to be rolling around in one continuous circle. He could not bring his thought processes to latch onto the idea that Bill Robertson and Deputy Mark Winslow were killed by the same man or for the same reason. Robertson had never been outside of Liberty, Texas for any length of time and his deputy was born and raised in Livingston County.

## **CHAPTER 11**

Parking in the small parking area at the end of the dam, Jonathan studied the perimeter of the lot as Chester came to join him. As it seemed to be a habit with him, Jonathan asked, "Where's Joseph?"

Pointing back up toward the tree line, Chester answered with a half grin. "Well Sheriff, like Joseph says, concrete parking pad 'ain't gonna give no clues' so he went back into the forest to see what the forest people can tell him."

Chester sounded just like Joseph. Jonathan knew that they would just have to wait until the red man came back out.

"Sheriff, you think the killings are all tied together with this Russian thing?"

"I don't know Chester, it could all be tied together. The airport security tapes should be here by morning. I want you and one of the deputies to scan the tapes looking for a familiar face. Check all rosters for passenger names for one that you might know."

"You think the killer is someone that lives here?"

"Yeah, Chester, I do. I also know it will be like looking for a needle in a haystack but our guy has to fly out and back if he is local. Being a small rural town, new folks are very noticeable. So, our perp comes breezing into a town just to waste someone and then breeze back out. Stranger coming into in a small town is noticeable no matter how hard someone tries not to be noticed, that old nosey lady down the street will see him."

Nodding, Chester speculated out loud, "Then it most likely is someone who has been here a while. Someone that does a lot of traveling so it would not be noticeable or of any concern to anyone that he or she is gone so much. Someone that people wouldn't pay much attention to if he is here for a day or two."

"Yeah, that about covers it, Chester. So, I'm hoping we might see his face in an unguarded moment on the airport terminal tapes."

Joseph chose that moment to walk out of the woods. Jonathan was not surprised that his deputy, as always, had critical information to add to the building case.

"Our shooter waited in the woods for Robertson, the perp walks in from a clearing where he or she parked their car out of sight. They waited and when Robertson came up top, the perp joins him. Robertson must have been expecting someone because he did not turn to face 'em."

Nodding, Jonathan had expected no less. Turning to Chester, he gave him new instructions, "Get the lab guys out to the parking area, Joseph will lead them there. Have them follow the trail and pick up anything that does not belong. Hopefully the tire tracks will be deep enough to get a plaster…"

Joseph interrupted Jonathan with the bad news, "The parking was paved, there were no marks."

"Damn," was the only reply from Jonathan but he did go on to say, "If there is a connection between our Russian, Robertson and Winslow, we have to find it. The more I think about it, the more I am beginning to think we have two separate cases."

The two deputies nodded, agreeing with the Sheriff but had little to add and whatever that would have been was interrupted by Jonathan's cell phone. Lillian's voice informed them.

"Sheriff have some information on the Robertson case, you may want to come in to review."

Jonathan's response was "10-4 Lillian". Looking at Joseph, his next words were hard to say out loud. "Start doing a check on our dead deputy, I want to know what life was like when he wasn't on duty."

Joseph opened his mouth to question Jonathan's instructions but quickly closed it He knew the answer to his own question. Who disliked Deputy Mark Winslow enough to kill him?

Seated at his desk, Jonathan was quiet as Lillian told him what was on the report she had just handed him.

"Mark Winslow was a cheating husband. Not just once, the nearest count I could get is three times. He began cheating on his wife three years ago. His last conquest seems to have been Robertson's widow. We were able to identify the first one as Susie Abbott, but the second one was a well-kept secret.

Mulling over what Lillian had just told him, Jonathan voiced the only question that was running around in his head.

"The Winslow's were the perfect couple, high school sweethearts, church goers, active in the community... What caused Mark to start playing around?"

Lillian tried not to laugh at his question but lost the battle, "Jiminy boss, you ain't that innocent!"

A little embarrassed, Jonathan managed a sheepish grin. "Yeah, I know it normally starts with the bedroom. But we're talking about a guy I would have sworn loved his wife and was devoted to her. Not a guy who went looking for greener pastures."

Lillian nodded, she, too, thought the same thing but if that was true then why would Winslow go looking for other women?

Simultaneously Jonathan and Lillian blurted out, "Wife was cheating first!"

"That still doesn't give us a reason for killing him. If they both were paying around why would you kill the other?" Lillian questioned.

"The answer could be the second woman." Jonathan told her adding, "The spouse of the second found out his wife was cheating on him and went crazy. Instead of killing her, he kills the guy."

"Ok, so how do we find out the name of the third woman?" was Lillian's question.

Leaning back in his chair, Jonathan took a deep breath, answering her question, "How much you want to bet that one of our widows knows the name?"

"Now that's a bet I'd make. One of them knows but how do we find out?"

"That is an easy one Lillian, we simply ask them." Jonathan informed her as he stood. "And I might as well start asking now."

Standing, Lillian shook her head telling him, "That's a job I don't envy."

"Well that's too bad, because you are going to see the Winslow widow and I'm taking the Robertson widow. When you are talking to the widow, be sure and not let her know that the Robertson widow is being asked the same questions."

## **CHAPTER 12**

Seated in the living room of the Robertson home across from the beautiful widow, Jonathan could not help but notice the stress lines that had marred the widow's face on his last visit were gone.

"Would you like a cup of coffee Sheriff?" Her soft-spoken question interrupted Jonathan's thoughts, bringing him back to why he was there.

"Thank you but no, Mrs. Robertson..."

"Sheriff," Wendy Robertson once again interrupted Jonathan, "before you ask me whatever it is you came here to talk to me about please allow me to give you information I think will answer your questions before they are asked."

Jonathan was a little surprised but managed a nod and sat back in the King-Louie-the-whatever velvet chair.

"Bill and I had a public face, one of a loving and caring couple. Our private face was much different." Speaking in a softer tone, Wendy Robertson continued, "Bill was a very dull man and even duller in the bedroom, he tried but…" Her words trailed off as she paused to take a deep breath before continuing. "Bill and I were high school sweethearts. We were married when we were eighteen. It was not long before we both discovered we were not the mate the other was looking for. There has never been a divorce in my family and I was not going to be the first one, so I allowed Bill his fringe benefits. His affairs never lasted long and I didn't care anymore. I only asked that he keep his affairs quiet. I could pretend in the public eye that I was a happily married woman. And Bill allowed me the same. Believe it or not Bill and I were happy being together, our marriage had become more of friends living together than husband and wife." Pausing once again, she offered Jonathan a cup of coffee. When he shook his head 'no' she continued.

"The day Bill was shot and killed, he and I had a long talk about where our lives were going and what each of us wanted. Bill, it seems, was in love with his latest conquest and he wanted to marry her. He wanted a divorce. I was shocked, stunned to be exact. I never expected Bill would ever want a divorce, it would not fit his spotless reputation."

Wendy Robertson's laugh was soft but held very little merriment. Shaking her head, she got to her feet, walked slowly over to the front window and stood looking out. Jonathan remained quiet, allowing her whatever time she needed.

Turning to face him, the smile on her face was full of joy, "But, I told him he could have his divorce, I didn't care." Walking back over to the sofa, she sat down saying, "Bill was going to get a divorce but there was nothing else he would get. His properties, his money, this house, his fancy cars, all of it would be mine."

Understanding the look of doubt on his face, Wendy told him, "Two months ago Bill came home three sheets to the wind, as my daddy would have said. He was silly drunk and wanted to play so we played make a baby, I'm pregnant. My cheating husband is asking for a divorce so he can marry his new love and his wife is pregnant. What do you think a judge would have to say about that Sheriff?"

Standing Jonathan had to give the lady her due. She had played her husband. Putting his Stetson back on, he turned and walked to the door as he answered her question.

"Well I would say the judge would be granting you just about anything you asked for." Turning back to face her, he held his hand out. When she took it, he smiled saying, "You have any questions just let me know."

For the first time, Wendy Robertson's smile reached her eyes, "I will and thank you Sheriff."

Watching Patricia Winslow pouring a freshly made cup of coffee, Lillian was having trouble seeing this elegantly posed woman as a killer but her mama had always told her to never judge a book by its cover.

"I am sorry to be imposing on you, Mrs. Winslow, but the procedures have to be followed in this type of tragedy."

"It is alright, Lillian, I understand. And please call me Patricia."

"Thank you, Mrs... Patricia." Taking a short breath, Lillian asked, "When was the last time you spoke with Mark?"

Patricia Winslow took a sip of her coffee before answering, "The morning he left to go to work."

"Do you know of anyone who would want your husband dead?"

Shaking her head, the widow forced a small smile, answering, "No, everyone loved Mark. Perhaps, everyone but those he had arrested in the past."

Pausing for a moment, Lillian reminded herself to watch for tell-tale signs of someone lying before she asked, "Was your marriage having any kind of problems, Patricia?"

The widow's reaction was not what Lillian had expected, "Of course we had problems, what married couple doesn't? Would I want to see him dead? Absolutely not."

Patricia Winslow never blinked an eye, never paused for a breath, had no hand or facial tremors. Lillian had no doubt that Patricia Winslow would have passed any lie detector test but should there have been absolutely no tell-tale signs of stress? With that thought in mind, Lillian asked, "Was Mark having or had ever had an affair?"

This time there was a flicker, the pulse in the side of the woman's neck gave a slight bounce as well as a small quiver in her left hand. Taking the next step really wasn't easy for Lillian but she pressed forward. "Patricia when did Mark have an affair?"

Patricia Winslow's voice was slightly lower as she gave the answer for which Lillian was holding her breath.

"A year ago, but Mark ended the affair himself. He realized it was a mistake and that he loved me."

"Who was the affair with?"

Hesitating for a second, the answer was given slowly, "Mark never told me who but I always figured I knew."

"Patricia, I need to know the name of anyone who you think it might have been."

"If Bill Robertson had not been killed, I would have told you that it was Wendy Robertson."

To say she was somewhat surprised was an understatement, but Lillian managed to restrain a hasty conclusion as she inquired, "What made you think Mark was having an affair with Wendy?"

"Mark and Bill could not stand being anywhere near the other. Mark did not have a decent word to say about Bill. It had to be something serious or Mark would have acted differently. He was not a man to hold a grudge."

Pausing to gather her thoughts, Lillian finally asked, "Did you ever say anything to Wendy Robertson?"

"What would I have said to her?" the Winslow widow's voice was small.

In for an ounce, in for a pound as her mama also used to say. Lillian gave a short laugh that sounded more like a snort, expressing herself spontaneously, "Hell, I would ask her if she was screwing around with my husband."

Despite the seriousness of the moment, Patricia Winslow was unable to hold back her laughter at the shocked expression that was on Lillian's face. Not only was Lillian shocked at her remark she was really having a hard time not joining in the laughter with the widow.

Once her laughter was under control, Patricia Winslow surprised Lillian even further by telling her, "As a matter of fact, Lillian, that is exactly what I did ask her about ten days ago."

This shocked Lillian to the point that she went deadly quiet as she asked, "And what did Ms. Robertson say?"

"Well, her being a lady, she did refrain from using profanity, she assured me that in no way was she having an affair with my husband."

"Did you believe her?"

"I did not. I was not raised on a turnip farm, the hot rush of blood to her cheeks was all the proof I needed."

"What did you say to her then?"

"I told her to dump the SOB or I would sue her and take everything she owned or hoped to own. And I would see to it that every nasty, dirty, little piece of crap I could find on her and her husband would be plastered all over the social media that she is so into, as well as the press."

Lillian was stunned at the brutal honesty of Patricia Winslow and wasn't sure how she should proceed. So, taking a deep breath, she stood up and as calmly as she was able to manage, bid her a good day.

Sitting in her car, Lillian was a little slow starting it as the words that came out of Patricia Winslow's mouth played again in her head. She was not altogether sure what to think of the Winslow widow. It certainly was what she had previously thought. No way... she was the sweet, refined, soft-spoken, gracious woman she appeared to be. But was she capable of murder?

## **CHAPTER 13**

Parked down the street from the Kullpepper house, Jonathan glanced at his watch. Christopher Kullpepper was a stickler for time. It was now eight forty-five and if he kept to his schedule, Kullpepper should be leaving his house in exactly fifteen minutes. True to form, he walked out of the house got into his car, backed out of the driveway and drove off.

Starting his car, Jonathan moved slowly down the street and parked in front of house, curbside. Cathy Kullpepper had left for school forty-five minutes earlier. She had caught the school bus right in front of the house, at least he would not have to worry about her coming in while he was talking to her mother.

Ringing the doorbell of the Kullpepper house, Jonathan had little time to wonder if he was about to make a mistake before the door opened and Elizabeth Kullpepper smiled at him and warmly welcomed him.

"Sheriff Lawrence, what a surprise! To what do I owe for this visit?"

Removing his hat, Jonathan's answer was brief, "I need to talk with you, Mrs. Kullpepper, about your daughter."

Elizabeth Kullpepper gasped, "Cathy?" There was a catch in her voice. "Has something happened? She just left for school a few minutes ago."

"Mrs. Kullpepper, Cathy is okay. May I come in for a few moments?"

Stepping back from the doorway, Elizabeth took a deep breath before saying, "Of course Sheriff, excuse my rudeness but you startled me."

Following Elizabeth Kullpepper into a small fashionably furnished sitting room, Jonathan sat down across from her. Knowing there was no good way to phrase his questions, he took a deep breath and asked,

"Mrs. Kullpepper, how long has your husband been abusing your daughter, Cathy?"

The stunned expression on Elizabeth Kullpepper's face and the sudden drain of the blood from it was all the proof

Jonathan needed. As she opened her mouth to speak, Jonathan stopped her.

"Please don't deny it Mrs. Kullpepper, your face says it all. Just tell me why you did not go to the police or Child Protective Services?"

It took her several moments before she managed to speak past the racking sobs, "I…I didn't …know…not until…Cathy's …last birthday…" The sobbing was racking her body, making it even more difficult to speak. Jonathan sat quietly, giving her time to regain some control of herself. Finally, able to speak again, she told him, "When I went screaming to my husband, I told him I was going to report him to the authorities. He slapped me, knocking me down, he was like a madman. He told me he would kill me and Cathy before he would let me destroy his life."

Blowing her nose on a Kleenex from a box on the end table next to the sofa she was sitting on, Elizabeth Kullpepper's spine seemed to straighten as she put the soiled tissue in her pocket. When she raised her eyes to meet Jonathan's, her voice was steady as she asked, "What happens now?"

Jonathan ignored her sorrowful look, took his phone off his belt clip and pushed Lillian's number. When she answered, he told her, "Take one of the female deputies from juvenile and go pick up Cathy Kullpepper from Central High. Take her to Dr. Phyllis Jamison's office, she is to do a complete physical. Once that is done take her back to juvenile and retain her. Under no circumstance is anyone to see or talk to her except you and the deputy."

If Lillian was stunned or had any questions, she let it pass and merely acknowledged with a simple, "Yes sir."

Disconnecting, Jonathan tried to soften his tone of voice but was unsuccessful. There was not a doubt in him that Elizabeth Kullpepper knew her daughter was being abused.

Standing he informed her, "Mrs. Kullpepper you need to get yourself an attorney. I'll expect you and your attorney in my office by three this afternoon."

Not waiting for her to reply, Jonathan walked out. Once again taking his phone he pushed Joseph's number. When he answered, Jonathan told him, "Meet me at Kullpepper's office ASAP."

Joseph replied, "On my way."

Entering the third floor of the Chambers building, Jonathan and Joseph greeted the young receptionist with a nod. Jonathan spoke saying, "Sheriff Lawrence and Deputy Skywolf to see Mr. Kullpepper."

Standing, the receptionist smiled apologetically, "I'm sorry Sheriff but Mr. Kullpepper is in a very important meeting…"

Jonathan did not wait to hear the rest of the receptionist's speech, he walked around the desk and into Kullpepper's office. Kullpepper was, indeed, in the middle of a meeting and when Jonathan and Joseph came barging in, he sprang to his feet demanding, "What the hell is the meaning of this Sheriff?!"

Not pausing, Jonathan walked around Kullpepper's desk, grabbed him by the shoulder and spun him around until he was face down on his desk. Taking the handcuffs Joseph held out to him, Jonathan's voice was hard and cold as he spoke, "Mr. Kullpepper, you are under arrest for sexual and physical assault of a minor female identified as your daughter, you have the right to remain silent…"

Kullpepper's voice rose about five times louder as he shouted, "Unhand me, I'll have your badge…"

Yanking Kullpepper to stand up, Jonathan warned, "Mr. Kullpepper you have the right to remain silent. I suggest you comply before I slam my fist down your throat."

Taking him by the arm, Jonathan forced him to walk toward the door ignoring the three other men sitting stunned in front of Kullpepper's desk. As Joseph passed by following Jonathan, he tipped his hat saying, "Gentlemen, this meeting is adjourned."

## **CHAPTER 14**

In Jonathan's office, waiting for the attorney, Kullpepper was smiling at the Sheriff and Joseph, who were seated across the desk.

"Did I pull one on the big bad law dog?" he asked Joseph, who nodded answering, "Heap big law dog."

Feeling a little embarrassed, Jonathan admitted, "I had thought about for a moment. I would have waited to arrest him until no one was around but then I would have most likely broken every bone in his body."

Nodding, Joseph understood, "So, when he gets his lawyer, you going to interview him?"

"Yeah, I'm letting him stew a while in the holding cell. I want to hear from Dr. Jamison. The booking will take a while, I let them know it needed to go really slow and smooth."

"What about the wife?" Was Joseph's next question.

Leaning back in his chair, Jonathan shook his head giving a soft curse, "Damnit. That woman had to have known what was happening. She couldn't be that naive."

Standing, Jonathan instructed Joseph "Get a warrant and search the Kullpepper home. Pay close attention to the daughter's room. If you find anything at all that helps us build a solid case, bring it in."

Turning to leave, he stopped and turned back, telling Joseph, "Take a female deputy with you. A woman's eyes and her instincts will be better in a case like this."

As Jonathan walked out, Joseph picked up the phone to check on which female deputy would be available.

Sitting across the table from Elizabeth Kullpepper and her attorney, Peter Jennings, Jonathan wondered at the lack of compassion he had for this abused woman. He knew full well it was due to the fact that Elizabeth Kullpepper had known and did nothing to stop her husband's physical and sexual abuse of her daughter. For how many years, that was the question he wanted answered.

"Mrs. Kullpepper, you and I both know that you were aware of what your husband was doing to your child."

Jennings shook his head, interrupting him, "That is an assumption, Sheriff."

Nodding, Jonathan agreed, "You are right counselor, so let me make sure your client understands where I'm coming from."

Focusing his eyes directly on Elizabeth Kullpepper, he was blunt, "Mrs. Kullpepper, if you want any hope of ever seeing your daughter again," Jonathan, ignored Jennings who opened his mouth to voice another objection, he continued, "and to avoid being charged as an accomplice in allowing your daughter to be abused, you will write out a statement. That statement will cover when it was you, and I use that word loosely, *stumbled* upon the fact your husband was sexually assaulting your daughter and why you did not file charges on him and remove yourself and your daughter from him."

Trying to hold back her sobs, she managed to say, "He…said… he would kill us." By now Elizabeth Kullpepper's body is racked with sobs.

Glancing at the attorney, Jonathan rose saying, "Councilor, I suggest you take a few moments to get your client under control and go over what I have said."

With that, Jonathan walked out, turned and walked down the hall to the second interrogation room where Kullpepper was waiting with his attorney, Marvin Hatcher. Sitting down across from the two men, Jonathan did not mince words.

"Mr. Kullpepper, before you start denying the charges against you, let me make you aware that my lab is, at this moment, searching and combing your house for the tiniest piece of evidence. Also, your wife Elizabeth is in an interrogation room, writing out a statement as to how long this has been going on. How you have threatened to have her and your daughter killed if either of them opened their mouths." Looking directly at Hatcher, Jonathan told him, "I would suggest your client consider confessing and throwing himself on the mercy of the court."

Kullpepper, who remained quiet, looked at Jonathan with pure hate burning his eyes. He asked, "And what kind of deal do you suggest I ask the court for?"

There was no warmth in Jonathan's voice as he answered. "Well, personally I suggest you ask for a jail cell on the moon. Because whatever sentence you talk the court into giving you, your life is going to become a living hell when your cellmates are introduced to you."

The ringing of his cell phone caused Jonathan to get up and walk out before the attorney or Kullpepper could make a reply. Jonathan answered his phone as he walked out. "Lawrence."

"Sheriff, this is Curtis, I have something I think you need to see."

Walking into the tech room where Curtis and two other deputies are watching the Houston airport embarking and disembarking passengers Jonathan asks, "What have you got, Curtis?"

"Well Sheriff, while the others were watching the Houston video tapes, I got to thinking maybe our boy didn't leave by the way of Houston. So, I started with smaller airports that might have connections that could take our perp where he wanted to go."

Nodding, Jonathan agreed, "Not a bad idea, Curtis but that's going to leave a broader field."

Some of Curtis' excitement was beginning to show, "Yes sir, that's why I narrowed it some, to the closest small airfields like Waco or Galveston."

The big smile spread across Curtis' face told Jonathan all he needed to know, "OK Curtis, show me what you found."

"A very interesting face Sheriff."

Turning the monitor around just enough so that Jonathan had an un-obstructed view, Curtis leaned back and waited for his boss' response, and he was not disappointed.

"Damn!" was spat out in surprise by Jonathan. Looking at Curtis he asked, "Is this the one and only?"

Shaking his head, Curtis' fingers typed in rapid speed, bringing up two more shots saying, "No sir, and they are all on the day before and day after each of the shootings. Taking the plane from Waco he goes to Austin, then from Austin to Santa Fe, and from Santa Fe to wherever he needs to settle. It's a few hours extra traveling but it hid his trail pretty good."

Jonathan smiled at Chester, patting him on the back saying, "But not good enough." Straightening, Jonathan paused a moment before saying. "We still have unanswered questions and I keep wondering what did the report on CR 214 Bridge had to do with anything? And let's face it, Zachery Golightly does not give the appearance of a cold-blooded murderer. I would say he looks more like a man that would pay to have it done. He might even watch it being done. He doesn't have the physical strength to carry out a couple of those killings."

"So, you think there is an actual assassin and Mr. Golightly is the one giving him his orders?"

"Yeah, that's what I'm thinking. But I am also thinking, how do we get Golightly to give the guy up? Otherwise all we've got are coincidences." Was Jonathan's answer.

Curtis remained quiet, mainly because he did not have an answer to the Sheriff's question. He knew the sheriff would come up with some kind of plan. He was not disappointed as Jonathan instructed him, "Get a hold of Phil Sheridan at the FBI, tell him I need a deep, and I mean deep, background check on Golightly. I want to know every freckle on his body."

"Will do, Sheriff," pausing for a moment, Curtis said, "You know he's going ask why."

Nodding, Jonathan knew, "And you are to tell him that we believe Golightly is our Russian spy, nothing else, just that."

Leaving Curtis, Jonathan was met in the hallway by Elizabeth Kullpeppers' attorney, Peter Jennings.

"Sheriff, my client would like to speak with you." Not sure what Jonathan was opening his mouth to say, Jennings added, "Mrs. Kullpepper has calmed down, she would like to say a few words to you."

Nodding, Jonathan followed the young attorney into the interrogation room where Elizabeth Kullpepper was waiting. Sitting down across the table from her, Jonathan waited for her to speak. In a voice tight with restraint, she made a final plea.

"Sheriff, my sister Florence Bishop and her husband, Eugene, live in Colorado City. They have no idea of what has been going on with me and my husband. They love Cathy and would welcome her into their home. They are good people Sheriff and Cathy has always loved them. Please send Cathy to them, let them help her heal."

Shaking his head, Jonathan almost felt some pity as he told her, "Wherever Cathy is sent is not up to me, it's up to Child Welfare and the Probate Court."

With a shaking hand, she reached across the table, grabbing one of Jonathan's hands, "Please Sheriff, please…" At this point, Elizabeth Kullpepper once again broke down into loud, uncontrollable sobs. Removing his hand from her grasp, Jonathan stood and said, "I will give your sister's name to the court, they will investigate and make their determination."

Unable to speak, she nodded her head and tried to rise but Jonathan turned, telling her attorney, "Have her write her statement then we will book her. I imagine you will get bond before the days end." He walked out, not waiting for a reply.

## **CHAPTER 15**

Jonathan walked back into his office where Joseph was waiting. Sitting down at his desk across from Joseph, he took out a small black notebook. Opening the journal that Cathy Kullpepper had written in for the past five years, his face was cold, his lips set in a hard line. Finishing the last page, he closed the book slowly and looking at Joseph, he shook his head and spoke through gritted teeth. "I should have killed the SOB instead of arresting him."

"That would have been too quick. I just want to make sure we get to pick his cell mate." Was Joseph's reply.

Nodding, Jonathan agreed, "Yeah, shooting him would have been too quick of a way for him to die. Cathy's diary will be the nail that puts him in hell for at least the next twenty years of his miserable life. Only thing wrong with that, twenty years isn't long enough."

Nodding, Joseph changed the subject, "Where are we on this Russian thing?"

Jonathan quickly brought him up to date on Curtis' findings. "Sheridan is digging into Golightly's background, hoping to find some tie back to Russia."

"You gonna let him know we are on to him?"

"Not yet. All we have is his travels and there will be a hundred-and-one reasons for those trips presented by an attorney. No, we need the hired assassin."

Leaning back, Joseph smiled saying, "Well, we are back to square one. We give Golightly a target."

Nodding, Jonathan agreed, "We have not held that press briefing I promised, so we call it, parade James out for the photographers and hope that we spot the guy before he puts a slug in James." Pausing for a moment, Jonathan added, "And that's why I want you holding the press-conference. I am going to station myself on the courthouse roof. Sniper training comes in handy at times."

"Yeah," giving Jonathan a slight smile, he added, "On the ground we spot the perp, you take him out."

"If he raises a gun to fire, yeah. Hope you or one of the other deputies will be able to take him down before it comes to that."

Standing, Joseph told Jonathan "While you set up our Judas goat, I'm going to see what I can find out about Golightly from some of our shadow friends. The DA has to have some hidden secrets waiting to escape."

Walking to the door, Jonathan wished Joseph luck, "Golightly didn't drink, use drugs or fool around on his wife. He has a lily-white reputation as far as this town is concerned. So, I wish you luck."

Leaving his office, Jonathan drove home. He wanted to talk to Samantha. He had made his mind up about his next career move and he wanted to be sure his wife would be all right with his decision.

Samantha was in the kitchen, which seemed to be her favorite place to be whenever she was home. Giving Jonathan a big smile, she walked over to meet him, giving him a soft, swift kiss.

"Well this is a pleasant surprise, you playing hooky from work?"

Giving her a hug, he answered. "For an hour or so. Thought I would come home and have a cup of coffee with you."

Stepping back, she studied him quietly for a moment then turned and walked over to the pot of freshly made coffee. Taking two cups down from the cupboard, she said, "Sit down and let's skip the silly banter so you can tell me what's on your mind."

Jonathan waited until Samantha had placed a steaming cup of black coffee in front of him and sat down across from him.

"Elections are in five months and I am not planning on running for re-election. I have been mulling it over for a while. What I would want to do for the rest of my life, besides loving you."

Samantha bit down of her bottom lip, trying hard not to let the tears pooling in her eyes overflow. She was proud of the fact she also kept quiet, allowing him to continue.

"The mustang ranch has always been a dream and I can't see how there could be a better beginning than it has now. I also love working with the law but there is only so much a small-town sheriff can do. The idea that the Governor planted in my brain is not a new one. I've rattled that idea around for several years. He just lit the fuse. But I've got to know, will you be able to deal with it?"

Taking a sip of her coffee, Samantha took time to retain control of her emotions before answering. "The Governor has awakened some fire in you and when you asked me what I thought of the whole crazy idea, I told you how I felt. I told you I am supportive of whatever decision you make. That has not changed. I love you and your happiness is all I want."

Pausing, she took a deep breath, slowly releasing it before continuing, "Understand that I have one demand, and is not open for discussion, you will be at home when our child is born. You will remain at home for the first three months. And you will spend birthdays, Christmases, and graduations at home."

Holding up a forefinger, as he started to speak, she continued, "And your offices will not be in some office flat in Houston or Dallas or anywhere but right here in this small, rural town and I will interview, hire and oversee office personnel. Your agents are your responsibilities."

Giving him a big smile, she informed him, "You may speak now."

Now came Jonathan's turn to fight to keep the tears from overflowing. Standing, he walked around the table, took hold of her shoulders, and pulled her to her feet. Pulling her into his arms and holding her tight against him, he managed to say, "You got a deal."

Leaving the sheriff's office, Joseph knew more about Golightly than Jonathan. He had been hearing gossip from some of the reservation Indians for several years. Nothing that would bring the law down but enough that it could have ruined any chance of becoming the County Attorney, had it been repeated. But his Indian brothers didn't care what the DA did in his personal life as long as it did not infringe on handing out fairness to the Indian that came before him.

Joseph's first stop was at a small wooden cabin set back in the deep East Texas Forest a few yards from the tributary of the Trinity the natives called Rosa Pua (white water). He had never understood why it was called white water until his first experience with the rapids on a rampage.

Opening the door of the truck, he froze at the deadly sound of a rifle being cocked. Joseph froze and slowly he began raising his hands as he asked softly, "Is this how you greet your *Pabi*?" (brother)

It was several seconds before Joseph received a reply "Your mode of transportation has changed, Brother."

Joseph lowered his hands and stepped away from his truck. Turning to face Rosa Tseena (White Wolf), Joseph knew the reference of transportation was about the fact that whenever he had paid his brother a visit in the past, it had always been by canoe and never by sheriff's department vehicle.

Rosa Tseena stood well over six feet. He was muscular and dark skinned with long black braids and equally black as coal eyes. He was dressed totally in deerskin from his boots to the fringed shirt, except for the twenty-first century black 30/30 rifle held in his hand. The old west savage stood majestically before him.

"Didn't have time to waste on paddling a canoe, this isn't a pleasure visit." Joseph told him as he stepped forward. He held his hand out for a white man's handshake.

A slow smile twisted White Wolfs' lips as he gripped Joseph's hand, firmly telling him, "I figured as much but couldn't help but to raise the hairs on the back of your neck."

Not waiting for a reply, he turned, leading the way into the cabin. Pointing to a small wooden table and chairs next to a red brick fireplace, he told Joseph, "Have a seat I'll pour us a couple of cups of coffee."

Sitting down, Joseph looked around the cozy cabin in admiration. If you didn't know what to look for you would almost swear it was furnished in authentic old west style. But, if one were to look behind the seven-foot oak cabinet doors, they would find a modern-day refrigerator. Beneath the oak countertop that held a dish washing pan, you would find a modern-day cupboard of canned goods and snacks. Yes, in many ways his brother was a fraud, until it came to defending his friends, family and country, then he was a true savage.

Sitting two cups of steaming coffee down, Wolf sat down across from Joseph and saying, "Tell me what brings you to see me?"

Fifteen minutes later, Joseph sat back and waited for Rosa Tseena to make some sort of a reply. He was not disappointed.

Shaking his head, Rosa Tseena rose to his feet and walked over to the get the coffee pot. Returning to pour a fresh cup for Joseph before saying, "From what I see, you got a snake by the tail and your county attorney is that snake. A couple of times I've come close to removing his liver with my knife but because he looks sideways at some of our brothers and lets them slide on some minor damages, I control my urges."

"So, what made you want to remove our county attorney's liver?" Joseph wanted to know.

"He was a defiler of young women. Many of our native families are poor and some go to bed at night hungry. Golightly paid the fathers for a night with the young women. Of course, the Res police could never claim rape because the young women would agree to do it. It was to feed their mamas and the smaller children. I told the reservation leaders if they did not stop him, I would slit his throat. They relayed my message, the visits stopped and he continued to go light on my brothers."

Draining the last few drops of coffee left in his cup, Joseph stood up saying, "Wolf, thank you for the information. I will use it wisely."

Nodding, Wolf walked him to the door with Joseph acknowledging his trust, "I know you will Joseph and I hope you hang this snake."

Opening the door, the two men walked out into the mid-afternoon sun. Walking over to his car, Joseph asked a question he had often thought but never voiced.

"You've heard of Jonathan's ranch and what he is doing with the mustangs. Since you've been back, why have you not come and had a look?"

Shaking his head, Wolf knew Joseph well enough to know there was another question below this one so he answered both with one reply.

"I paid a visit and I have been observing, just have not chosen to speak to Tosahwi as yet."

Getting in the car, Joseph rolled the window down as he closed the door and asked the one other question he wondered about.

"Why do you call him Tosahwi, the White Knife?"

Smiling, Wolf stepped back shaking his head and saying, "that you must ask Tosahwi himself."

Knowing it would do little good to argue the point, he turned the key, threw the shift into reverse and headed back to the courthouse, vowing he would remember to ask Jonathan what was the meaning of the name Tosahwi between him and White Wolf.

## **CHAPTER 16**

Lying flat on the roof of the courthouse, Jonathan scanned the gathering crowd standing at the bottom of the courthouse steps. He was a bit surprised at the number of people who were gathering there, waiting for word on the school shooter. Sanchez and Curtis were on the sidelines, videoing the faces and being as inconspicuous as possible, which was quite difficult. Moving the scope, Jonathan studied each face. Many he recognized as locals, his deputies, and a couple of Sheridan's men. There were also several press representatives from newspapers as well as television.

With the opening of the courthouse door, Joseph stepped out and the group of reporters began shouting questions. He had James with him in handcuffs, Joseph held up his left hand, asking for silence. Jonathan could not help but to smile at Joseph's obvious point of holding his left hand up. He left his gun hand, the right hand, free. Moving the scope off of Joseph and James, he once again started a slow scan. The earpiece in his right ear enabled him to hear not only the deputies, but also some of the crowd's comments as he scanned past them.

Stopping on the face of a tall, scruffy looking man in a cheap plaid jacket, Jonathan recognized him as a man that usually hung around the local beer joints. Jonathan was also aware that the scruffy guy was an undercover Texas Ranger who just happened to be in town and offered to be in the crowd. It was an offer Jonathan had graciously accepted. Slowly, Jonathan moved the scope over the crowd as Sheridan's voice sounded in his earpiece.

"Sheriff, your man Golightly is in cuffs and on his way to the Federal court," Jonathan's single thought was "one down, one to go." The sudden soft utterance of "gun" jerked Jonathan back to the present as he swung the scope to the scruffy guy in the plaid jacket who was pointing toward a man in a black cap, black leather jacket and dirty blue jeans. He was standing across the street from the courthouse and was in the process of raising his rifle, which was pointing toward the handcuffed James who was standing next to Joseph. It took seconds for Jonathan to squeeze the trigger of the sniper rifle he held over from his Chicago days.

At the sound of the rifle, Joseph dove to the ground pulling James with him. Curtis and Sanchez swung their video cameras, capturing the scene of the deputies in the crowd running toward the fallen triggerman. Frenzied, the small crowd began running away from the courthouse, seeking shelter.

Rising to his feet, Jonathan did not wait for a deputy to signal that the shooter was dead, he had made that shot too many times not to know the guy was dead.

An hour later Joseph, Curtis, Sheridan and Jonathan were sitting in the Sheriff's office. It did not take thirty minutes to run the shooters' prints on the national criminal and immigration fingerprint data base to score a hit and for Sheridan to read it aloud.

"Henri Schultz is an assassin listed as a guy who does selected jobs for the outed KGB. He free-lanced to the highest dollar."

"So, what happens to Golightly now? He walks because our one witness is dead?" Jonathan hoped he was going to like the answer Sheridan was about to share with him.

"Well with Schultz dead and only Golightly's trips as evidence… unless he comes clean, he will walk."

The harsh response from the Joseph let Jonathan and Sheridan know how he was feeling about Golightly walking.

Shaking his head at Joseph to stay calm, Jonathan studied Sheridan for several moments before responding.

"So, what are you not telling us Sheridan?"

Grinning, Sheridan knew that there was no way his friend, the Sheriff, would let Golightly walk away as a free man.

"Simmer down guys, remember we are on the same side of this." Laying a folder on Jonathan's desk, he told them, "Our friends the Russians want Golightly, and I figure your DA ain't gonna want to be sent back for his Russian buddies to pass on a little justice. Here in America he would be housed in a warm cell, fed three meals a day, light labor, maybe mopping the floors, a library, television and even a movie theatre. Oh yeah, he won't like the idea of going back to Mother Russia. Figure you can get him to tell you just about anything."

It had not taken Joseph more than a couple of seconds to catch onto Sheridan's statement and it brought a big smile to not only his face but also Curtis' and Jonathan's.

Standing, Jonathan looked at Curtis and told him, "Bring Golightly up from the cell block, put him in interrogation room one and lock him in. We'll leave him to sweat a little before talking with him. In the meantime, Phil and I need to have a private talk." Glancing from Curtis to Joseph, he added, "If you gentlemen will excuse us for a few minutes."

Waiting until the two were out of the room, Jonathan turned to Sheridan saying, "You can quit playing your damn games. You know sure as hell the feds are not going to let a small rural town sheriff have someone like Golightly." Jonathan was angry and it was evident in his tone.

Realizing it would do little good to stall his friend, he explained, "Golightly has names, names that we want. He didn't start eliminating these moles to protect his hide. The dead moles didn't even know Schultz was here. If the

Russians start appealing to our President and promising they will deal out justice to this murderer, the President will see it their way."

When Sheridan paused, Jonathan finished for him. "And by getting him to ask for asylum, we get to keep him."

Sheridan managed only half of a grin, this time not wanting to really tick his friend off.

"Actually, not you but me. We keep him, we stash him away, and we milk the information until there isn't any more."

Not liking the way things were going, Jonathan asked, "And what then, when the milk has dried up? You let him go?"

Sheridan's voice was cold as he answered, "Hell no. Then we send him home to Mother Russia."

Slightly stunned at the hatred in Sheridan's tone of voice, Jonathan understood the true meaning of vengeance. Nodding, he found himself agreeing with Sheridan and his logic, which brought another thought front and center. Motioning for Sheridan to sit down, Jonathan sat on the corner of his desk to ask Sheridan, "How would you like to go to work for the newly formed L & M Global Investigation firm?"

Before Sheridan could ask questions, Jonathan filled him in on the coming events. Finally, wrapping it up he said, "Think about it before you answer. You might even want to talk to your wife before answering."

Sheridan was silent for several moments before he asked, "What did Sam have to say about this?"

"Same thing your wife most likely will say. She doesn't like the sound of it, ground rules laid down and she says she can handle it if it's what I want."

"Yeah, that sounds like my wife. Standing, Sheridan held his hand out, taking Jonathan's in a firm handshake he told him, "I'll let you know by next week, after I talk to my wife." Walking to the door, he added, "I have to admit, it sounds like something I would want to be involved in. Either answer I give; I want you to know I appreciate the confidence you have shown you have in me by asking me to join."

Nodding, Jonathan opened the door to find Joseph and Curtis waiting outside. Smiling, he told them, "Okay boys, load up the boxes of evidence and pack it in Agent

Sheridan's trunk. Then escort Golightly out to the car in shackles and lock him in the back seat."

The two did not wait for further instructions. They turned and immediately went to carry out his orders. Sheridan and Jonathan waited for the two to bring Golightly out, then they followed them to the car. Sheridan opened the driver's side door, nodded toward the three men, Curtis, Joseph and Jonathan, got in and started the engine before driving out of the parking lot.

Glancing at the two deputies, Jonathan said, "Well friends, what say we call it a day and go home to our wives?"

## **CHAPTER 17**

On the drive home, Jonathan called Samantha to let her know he was on his way but that he wanted to take a ride before coming in. He wanted to do one little thing and asked her if she would like to join him. He was slightly disappointed when she said no and that she felt like he needed the time alone. Jonathan knew before that he loved Samantha but when she so softly told him she understood him so thoroughly and loved him despite his shortcomings, it was then Jonathan realized just how much she loved him.

The drive home took very little time and saddling his favorite blue roan mare took even less time.

Sitting atop a sloping hill that was covered in lush green grass and tall green pines, Jonathan was feeling blessed beyond words as he watched the small herd of mustangs on the valley floor. It had taken him a few years to shed the city chains but the past was behind him and so was the visitor who observed him from the tree line a few yards away. The rider had been there for the past twenty minutes and Jonathan figured it was time to make it known that he was aware of his presence. Without turning he asked, "I guess you've heard by now about your friend the DA?"

Rosa Tseena was the rider behind Jonathan. Once the silence was broken between the two, Rosa Tseena, White Wolf, touched his heels to the flanks of his mount, a beautiful sixteen-hands black stud, and moved to ride up beside Jonathan.

"That SOB is no friend of mine, as you well know, Sheriff." Was his reply. Jonathan smiled, nodding, "Yeah, I know, wasn't the punishment we planned but I guess it'll do."

Nodding, Wolf returned the smile. Pointing toward the herd, he said, "Your Aussie is a good man with a horse. Tosahwi, you need him here with these animals, not wandering all over the globe chasing bad guys."

Jonathan realized Wolf had a motive for his observation of Lucas and that was also the reason for his visit with him now. Jonathan had met Wolf three years before when Wolf had ridden up on him, just in time to help with freeing a horse's leg from a trap. Trying to calm the horse and pry the trap jaws open with a white pearl handled knife he had carried since age fifteen was proving to be too much. Wolf rode up on the horse's blind side, dropped a blanket over its head, and then swung out across the horse's neck, bringing it down in a pro-cow dogging style. The horse went down and Wolf lay across its neck, pinning it while Jonathan removed the trap. Jumping back, trap in hand, just as Wolf rolled off and away from the horse, the two stood and watched as the horse got up and galloped off.

Turning to face Wolf, Jonathan had held his hand out saying, "Thank you for your help. My name's Jonathan."

Wolf acknowledged Jonathan's introduction with a smile, telling him, "I know. You are Sheriff Jonathan Lawrence and this is your land. Well, Sheriff Jonathan Lawrence, I think I shall call you Tosahwi.

"Tosahwi, and what does that mean?" Had been Jonathan's one question. The answer left him somewhat confused.

"It means White Knife. You are the first man I have ever seen carry a pearl handled white knife. I am Rosa Tseena, White Wolf, we are brothers."

Three years later, the two had built up a strong though somewhat strange friendship. Jonathan knew Wolf had ridden to see him for a purpose and he was tired of waiting to learn what it was.

"What's on your mind, Wolf?" Jonathan was prepared for almost anything, but he had to admit, Wolf's next words surprised him.

"It is known because your deputy and friend, Joseph Skywolf, is also my blood brother and we talk especially when he has troubles on his mind. He tells me you are going to form a company that is not handicapped by the rule of written law but by the law of right. You will go after those that seek to destroy what others have built and have dreamed of. I have fought for those same rights many times but my footprint upon those rights have been small. I wish to be part of your team."

Holding his reply for several minutes, Jonathan was not ignorant of Wolf's history. The man had served twelve years with the Green Berets. He was a guerilla-fighter, equally as dangerous with a knife as with a gun. He had joined the service at eighteen and had been honorably discharged at age thirty after being severely wounded in his chest. The bullet had clipped his left lung and had earned him his discharge papers.

Jonathan knew there could be no better man to have at his back. Including Wolf, they would number five, to begin the new challenges that were to come. There were still a lot of questions to be answered and plans to be made but Jonathan knew beyond a doubt that this is what he was meant to do. Only time would tell how things turned out but he would leave that to God to decide.

# MEET THE AUTHOR

## Sue Land

Sue Land is native Texan and is devoted to preserving Texas culture and history. She is an active historian and has written and been involved in filmmaking for more than twenty-five years. In addition to being the author of the *Digger* mystery book series, Sue is the Director and Producer for Swanee Productions, an independent film company, as well as the Director and Publicist for the Billy the Kid Museum in Hico, Texas.

Made in the USA
Las Vegas, NV
05 January 2025